QUAINT CITY

Three Stories of Queer Love

Avery Morstan

Individually, these ebooks were dedicated to my mother and my grandmother, Megan Gann and Bernadette, whose bangs I really did cut a hole in one afternoon at the salon where I worked.

In addition to these beautiful humans who support me, this author would also like to acknowledge the beta reading and light editing services of the following individuals: Megan Gann (she/her), Jenn Robinson (she/they), Allegra D'Ambruoso (she/her) and the Prophet Loki Sidhe Discord (they/them).

SEAMS A BIT QUEER

CHAPTER ONE

There was a very slight crack next to the boob-shaped overhead light in Kameron's room. She didn't know why so many lights in rental apartments were shaped like tits, but the hairline crack that radiated away from hers reminded her of a vein, pulsing outward. Kam would never have noticed the crack except for the fact that she'd been staring at her ceiling for the last half-hour with her stomach in knots trying to eat itself. She knew *why* she was avoiding the kitchen and she also knew that the same reason she was avoiding the kitchen was also the reason they probably didn't have anything to eat even if she *did* go in.

Fucking Kyle.

Her stomach growled loudly. She rolled over to her side and scrunched the pillow under her head. The situation was getting dire, then.

"Babe! You're out of cereal!" said a loud, jarring masculine voice. Kam cringed. The obnoxious voice that was practically screaming through her apartment didn't actually live here. Rather, he was romantically attached to her roommate, Scarlett, and Scarlett didn't eat cereal. Kam purchased and devoured cereal. Actually, it was one of her favorite foods. She could eat whole boxes of chocolatey rice puffs or frosted processed corn in one sitting, but it had been hard to keep on hand since Kyle had started staying with them during the pandemic.

So, what Kyle was *really* saying was that *Kam* was out of cereal.

Kameron puffed out a breath and her stomach growled again, this time louder.

"Babe! You're out of milk, too! And peanut butter!" Kyle called. Kam buried her face in her pillow and let out a groan of frustration. How could they be out of everything?

"Ew, what was that?" Kyle said, and he was clearly speaking to himself in the other room, but the apartment had some thin walls. Kam gritted her teeth. From Scarlett's room, she could hear the gentle hum of a vintage sewing machine and she knew that Scarlett probably couldn't hear Kyle's complaints over the noise of it. Or, if she could, she was choosing to ignore him and who could blame her? Kam actually enjoyed the machine's gentle thumping noise. It was a really nice sound to fall asleep to, unless Scarlett broke a needle because that was often followed by several loud curse words.

Sewing had been something that Scarlett learned over the course of the pandemic and she'd fallen absolutely in love with it. Kyle hadn't been living with them at first, and it had just been Kam and Scarlett, trying to keep each other sane during the mounting terror and uncertainty. Kam had done the queer thing and started baking obscene amounts of banana bread. Scarlett had done video chats with Kyle. And they'd bickered a little, probably just to break up the buzzing anxiousness and monotonous atmosphere. Finally, like every other household in America, they'd turned to learning hobbies.

Kam had ordered a crochet hook and some rainbow yarn from the local shop in order to make herself a pride-themed scarf for winter. Quaint City had a few cutesy shops and she wanted to keep the money local. Scarlett had been cruising an online yard sale group one day and found her vintage sewing machine, which was cheap but needed some oiling and cleaning because it had been in this guy's garage for a decade or two. The warm, golden afternoons that had seen Kam splayed across the foot of Scarlett's bed, hooking away, while Scarlett watched videos of how to get her darling Ruby (that's what she named her machine and it was precious) in proper working order, had been some of the happiest moments of Kam's life.

"Cause she's like my child," Scarlett had giggled, regarding the name of the machine. "So like Scarlett Junior, only she's precious, too, like a jewel. My Ruby."

Like most people of 2020, cloth masks had been one of Scarlett's first projects, and Kameron had a growing collection of them on her nightstand. There was one at the very top of the pile which was a black cotton with ditzy little flowers all over it that was her very favorite. It was the first one Scarlett had ever made.

"So you can be safe," Scarlett had told her, with a smile that lit up her whole face. Scarlett didn't just smile, she beamed, like a beacon, pulling everything around her closer with her warmth.

Without Kyle to interrupt her on the daily, Scarlett had managed to take her sewing to a whole other level when she started her side business, Ruby Stitches. She made these incredible flowy dresses in fun printed fabric that she continued to source online as more and more people cleaned out their garages. The whimsical caftans (because that was sort of how they looked, only caftan-but-make-it-fashion) had provided her a nice outlet for her creativity to flow and Kam took pictures of her modeling the garments on their fire escape or lounging in Scarlett's colorful room. Personally, Kam was a minimalist, and all of her furniture was clean lines and cubes from Ikea, but Scarlett had that vintage touch and it made her all the more magical. Ruby Stitches was growing into a solid side hustle and Kam was proud of Scarlett.

Sadly, she was the only one.

With restrictions loosening despite the virus continuing to rage, Kyle had become a permanent fixture in their apartment and the first thing he'd complained about, other than their lack of food, was the time Scarlett spent on her machine.

Kam huffed. She heard Kyle's loud, thumping footsteps make their way back to Scarlett's room and the humming of the machine stopped abruptly. There was a quiet murmuring, Scarlett's voice answering whatever he was saying, and then Kyle let out a whine.

"Babe, I'm gonna starve. Let's go," he complained.

Kameron couldn't quite make out Scarlett's reply, but Kyle's next remark made her jolt up in bed.

"You sew too much. It's not like this shit is ever going to make real money. I don't even know why you try."

"Alright, asshat, that's it-" Kameron growled to herself. Her feet hit the floor with a vengeful slap and she headed for the door. But just as her fingers curled around the knob, there was a gentle tap on the wooden panel from the other side. Kameron opened her door, and there was Scarlett. She'd been sewing, as evidenced by the stray threads clinging to her dress, and her red hair was pulled up into a messy bun on the top of her head, with curls springing out in frizzy tendrils.

"Hey, we're going to run to the grocery store, and then probably grab some pizza. Can I get you anything?" Scarlett asked. Over her shoulder, Kyle had stomped into Scarlett's room and closed the door. Kam sighed and Scarlett's face faded quickly from tired to embarrassed. "There *may* be a slight cereal shortage. I'll replace it, though."

Kameron could feel the buzzing anger under her skin, but she didn't want Scarlett to think that it was directed at her, so she just blew out a weary sigh and shook her head. She hoped that her face looked casual despite her frustration. "I'm good. I'll schedule a no-contact pick-up later for my stuff. Y'all have fun."

If it had been anyone other than Scarlett, Kam would've had something nasty to say about boyfriends who steal too much food, but with those big doe eyes on her, she couldn't bring herself to complain. Especially since Scarlett knew that Kyle and Kam didn't get along well and had tried to keep their interactions to a minimum. After that, what could Kam possibly say?

As Kam's eyes fell, unable to hold Scarlett's gaze any longer, she let herself focus more closely on what Scarlett was wearing. It was a loose, bright printed dress with cartoon mermaids all over it and a large, ruffled collar. The way the fabric brushed against Scarlett's rounded thighs and displayed the one large tattoo that Kameron knew about was delicious. Kam flushed and cleared her throat.

"I love that! Is it new?"

"Yeah! I made it yesterday!" Scarlett said excitedly, giving a little twirl that had the fabric flaring out around her. Kam pressed her lips together and tried to look *very* excited and not just turned on.

"That's amazing. You're so creative," Kam told her. She heard Kyle's condescending laugh and she looked over Scarlett's shoulder at him. He was leaning in the doorway with his arms crossed over his chest.

"Maybe half-creative. She probably copied that from someone she saw on the 'Gram," Kyle said with a mean smile. "I saw her searching *clowncore* yesterday-"

"Well, I love it. That collar is stunning," Kam said. She reached out to give Scarlett's hand a quick, reassuring squeeze. "I bet that took a lot of time to figure out."

"Yeah, it did," Scarlett said slowly. Kam didn't like how the excited light had faded out from Scarlett's eyes, and she wondered what else Kyle had voiced an opinion on when Kam wasn't within ear shot.

"Look, babe, are you ready to go? I'm hungry." Kyle pushed past them, wrapping an arm around Scarlett and dragging her away. Scarlett shot a glance over her shoulder at Kam, who tried not to interpret the emotion there as 'please rescue me, he's secretly a serial killer', and called back,

"I'll see you later, Kam!"

Kam watched them grab their masks and head outside. At least the apartment was safe now, for a little while. Maybe it was past trauma from when she was younger, or that she'd had some shitty roommates in her day, but when Kyle was around Kam just didn't want to leave her room. She felt stifled, barricaded, unable to get out of bed and listening to them bicker from behind the thin walls. His hyper-critical jokes didn't make Kam feel safe in her own apartment. Maybe it was time to think about moving out. But... that would mean leaving Scarlett on her own with that douchebag.

Kam padded out into the kitchen to see if there was anything left from Kyle's reign of refrigerator terror.

There wasn't.

She managed to make the world's most pathetic grilled cheese with two heels of bread and the one american cheese single left in the place, and it was just going to have to hold her until she was able to get some real food. She padded back to her room, plate in hand, but she paused just outside of Scarlett's door.

The sewing machine's front panel was open, and the bobbin casing was out, with the bobbin laying tangled in a heap. Prior to living here, Kam couldn't have told you what a bobbin was but after the crash course in sewing machine maintenance that Scarlett had gone through, she knew it was important to how the machine functioned. She couldn't imagine Scarlett leaving Ruby in such a state, but then again, Kyle *had* been particularly whiny today. Kameron frowned and left it. Not her machine, not her boyfriend and definitely not her Scarlett. She closed her bedroom door and ate her nasty grilled cheese and spent the rest of the day in her room. Alone.

The lovebirds returned, eventually, and their noises were almost impossible to drown out. It seemed like everything was a production with the two of them. Kam understood love, and she'd definitely played that whole 'opposites attract' game a few times in her life, but there were still limits. You still needed to be somewhat on the same page about basic household functions if anything was going to get done- like bringing in groceries or sorting out food. In an effort to drown out the chaos, Kam tried to nap and then gave up and pulled up her laptop. Her favorite romcom was available for streaming, she knew, and she was willing to doze along while it played.

About halfway through, there was a light knock on her door, startling her a bit, and then Scarlett let herself into Kam's bedroom.

"Can I come in?" she asked, giving Kam a hopeful smile.

She held a plate in her hands, with a few slices of pizza on it. "Brought you something to eat. I know you said you weren't really hungry earlier but I just thought you might like some. It's from that stoner place up the street that you like."

Kam paused the movie and sat up in her bed. Her hands reached up to scrub the bleariness out of her eyes because it looked an awful lot like an angel had just delivered pizza to her and the vision was too much not to be a dream. "Sure. Everything alright? Did Kyle go home?"

She scooched so her back was up against the wall, with her legs criss-crossed beneath her. She smiled as Scarlett handed her the pizza and slid up on the bed to join her.

"Oh, yeah, he's fine. He's in the living room playing that game he likes. I was trying to read but him and his friends get so loud even with the headphones that I can't sit there for very long," Scarlett told her. Kam shoved a piece of pizza in her face to avoid the disappointment that Kyle was still inhabiting their home.

"And Ruby isn't working."

"Your machine isn't working?" Kam asked, swallowing her pizza with a gulp. "It was fine earlier."

Scarlett sighed, her brows knitting together like she was still trying to puzzle out how it was working perfectly one second and then not working the next. "I know, I know, but the bobbin is skipping stitches and getting gnarled on the back of the fabric, so I can't finish that order I took for Gallery QC. At least, not until I figure out what's happening with it."

"Hey, I'm sure you'll figure it out. You got it working in the first place, didn't you?" Kam asked, nudging Scarlett with her elbow. Scarlett gave her a grateful smile.

"Yeah. It's- It's been a dream, being able to start this business. I'd like to stop teaching one day and just do this, but in this economy," Scarlett trailed off with a sigh. Kam looked down at her pizza, picking at the crust.

"Scarlett, if anyone can do it, I know you can," Kam told her. "You're determined, and you've got a good business sense. And your social media has been on point."

"Yeah, I know, it's just that Kyle-"

"Fuck Kyle," Kam said before she could stop herself. Scarlett giggled.

"I do."

"That's so gross," Kam groaned, and she pretended to gag. Scarlett laughed. It was the first real sound of joy that Kam had heard out of her in a long time.

"I thought I'd come see what you were up to. Maybe have a girl's night while he's exploring the wastelands or whatever in his game," Scarlett said.

"I'd really like that. We haven't had one of those in a long time," Kam said softly. She was painfully aware at how close Scarlett was sitting. Their legs were knocking together, and their shoulders were just a hair away from touching.

"Awesome!" Scarlett's focus turned to the laptop on Kam's bed. "So, what are we watching?"

"Oh, um. I was watching that one about the defunct rockstar who falls in love with Drew Barrymore. Because you know my thing about Drew Barrymore," Kam said, and she flashed a sideways smile at Scarlett. "Not to mention they're definitely a disaster queer couple. Can't convince me this is a hetero romance."

Scarlett beamed her sunshine-smile back. "Absolutely. Ten out of ten, one hundred percent agree. The way you find queerness in straight media has to be one of my favorite things about you."

"Well, it's not like we get a ton of representation. I've got to make do with what I've got," Kam said. She reached over and pressed play again and for a few minutes they were quiet. Just Kameron, definitely not thinking about how fucking *warm* Scarlett was. Not Kameron, feeling like sweat was beginning to pool at the base of her spine.

"I just don't understand how it could have broken so easily," Scarlett finally mumbled under her breath. Kameron glanced over at her.

"I'm not sure either. Leaving it open like that couldn't have been good for it," Kameron said, picking at the worn spots in her jeans. Scarlett frowned, with her brows knitting together.

"I didn't leave it open," she said.

"Sure you did. Your bedroom door was open when I came in and I saw the bobbin thing out and the door to the inside of the machine was open," Kameron told her.

Scarlett's face started to look like someone doing calculus. "But when we came back... I mean, I guess I was in the kitchen for a while, and Kyle was-"

Right conclusion reached, then. Kyle had done something to sabotage the machine.

"Well, don't jump to conclusions. Maybe it's just an old machine and it's high maintenance," Kameron told her, pursing her lips. She hated saying it but she knew if she said anything else she was going to say something along the lines of 'fucking dump him' and that would probably cost her a friend. It had before. And life without Scarlett just sounded bleak.

"You're right. You're absolutely right," Scarlett said, but there was hesitation in her tone. If it were possible, she seemed to shift closer and she lay her head on Kameron's shoulder. "You're a good friend, Kam."

Good friends probably didn't think so much about the soft curve of their other friends lips and what that might feel like against their own, especially straight friends with stupid boyfriends, but Kam still blushed at the compliment. "Thanks."

They stayed like that, pressed close on Kam's bed, occasionally roasting the mid-two-thousands fashion or the actors, until the movie was almost over. That was about when Kyle burst in, looking for Scarlett, just moments before the final payoff of a kiss between the two lovers.

Kam wondered if there were other "payoffs" that Kyle missed, too.

"There you are! You just disappeared on me," Kyle said, as if Scarlett had committed some horrible crime by leaving him in the living room.

"Oh, we got all caught up in watching this movie. It's one

of my favorites!" Scarlett told him. Kyle looked at the screen, paused in that pivotal, pre-kiss moment where the rockstar had finally gotten the girl back after their stereotypical break-up.

"Ew, that stuff is lame. There's no plot and it's all eye candy," Kyle scoffed. Of course he didn't like 'chick flicks'. Kameron wanted to point out the hundreds of scantily clad women in the video games that Kyle was obsessed with. How they never seemed programmed to fight as strongly as their male counterparts, all of whom were fully clothed. What were they there for, if not eye appeal? But, Scarlett was already scooting off the bed, and Kam felt a loss at her warmth.

"See you later, Kam," Scarlett said. "Sounds like it's this guy's bedtime."

Kyle grinned lecherously and Kam was just embarrassed for him. "Oh yeah, it's definitely past *bedtime*."

Once Scarlett was out of the room with Kyle and the door was firmly shut behind them, Kam let out a massive groan and flopped over on her bed. She could start a new movie… or just stare sullenly at her ceiling. Which seemed more likely.

CHAPTER TWO

Kameron's door creaked open and her head popped out, ready to pop back in at a moment's notice. The door across the hall was still closed, and there didn't appear to be anyone in the living room or kitchen. Hopefully, she could sneak out and then get back into her room before anyone made an appearance. She'd forgotten to schedule the pick up for groceries, and she was pretty sure nothing had materialized in the fridge, but she was willing to try. She padded down the hall, trying her best to be as quiet as possible.

"Yesssss," she hissed to herself as she reached to the top of the fridge, arm stretched and on tip-toes. Scarlett had performed a miracle and remembered to replace the cereal that Kyle had stolen. Mini-marshmallows would certainly brighten up Kam's Saturday immensely. She poured a bowl for herself, with milk as Scarlett had remembered to replace that, too. Kam sighed happily as she took her first bite.

Her joy was interrupted by the sound of Scarlett's door opening and closing.

Kam was prepared to run at the first sight of Kyle, but she was pleasantly surprised to see Scarlett. God damn, she was a sight in the morning. Her hair was still sleep-mussed, the curls falling softly down her back, and she had on an oversized blouse that looked loose and cool. The jeans she was wearing were light in color but had a stripe of darker denim running down the side, which looked really neat and highlighted the plush curve of her hips.

"New jeans?" Kam asked, glancing up to meet Scarlett's eyes. There was something there, like Scarlett had noticed Kam noticing, and enjoyed the slow appraisal. Kam started to blush. She felt caught, and maybe she was. She quickly crunched another spoonful of cereal.

"Old jeans, actually. I added the strip in," Scarlett said, and it was her turn to flush. She tucked a curl behind her ear. "I've gained a little, um, quarantine weight and I couldn't get them on without adding some panels."

"You look amazing. You did a great job," Kam said, praying there were no rainbow colored marshmallows sticking to her teeth. As usual, she was so focused on Scarlett, she hadn't heard the door to Scarlett's room open again, but there was Kyle coming into the kitchen. He looked less amazing. He hadn't bothered to get dressed and he was shirtless and in just his boxers. His hair was sticking up at all angles.

"Lemme get a bowl of that," he grunted, snatching the box of cereal from the counter. In a total dude-bro move, he tipped his head back and poured the cereal directly into his open mouth.

"Kyle, that's not ours," Scarlett told him.

"Um, I literally watched you buy it," Kyle said with flecks of hearts and horseshoes spraying out when he talked.

"Yeah, to replace what you ate. You can't take Kam's stuff," Scarlet pointed out, her eyebrows raised and her eyes wide. Her voice had all the qualities of a kindergarten teacher scolding a misbehaving child. As she spoke, Kyle sat the box back on the counter and gave Kam a doubting look, as if they were conspirators, and it took everything Kam had not to kick him out.

"You sure about that? Are you sure maybe you didn't eat it?" Kyle reached out and patted Scarlett on her hip. "You're the one that had to make yourself fat pants."

Jesus fucking Christ, Kyle.

Scarlett must have seen the murderous look on Kameron's face because she started waving over Kyle's shoulder, like she didn't want Kam to start a fight. Kyle, completely clueless, had already moved to look inside their empty refrigerator.

"Get a move on, babe. I'm gonna need breakfast before we

take our walk. Probably want something light for you, don't you think?" Kyle said. He closed the fridge with a pointed look at Ruby and then went back to the bedroom. Presumably to get dressed? One would hope.

"Sure. Yeah, whatever you want, babe. Be right there," Scarlett said weakly.

Kam had choices to make. She could outright complain about the guy, or she could just shut up and let Scarlett do her own thing. But she didn't understand what was so special about Kyle, body-shamer supreme and King of the Douche Canoes. Scarlett shouldn't have to put up with shit like this.

"I know, I know," Scarlett said with a heavy sigh, probably answering the look on Kam's expressive face. A poker player Kam was not. "I don't know what to do with him. He can be really awful sometimes, I guess."

"He is... pretty gross," Kam allowed herself to agree. She stirred her cereal, her appetite lost.

"But he can be really sweet. Or, he used to be kind of sweet. I think the pandemic has really gotten to all of us," Scarlett whispered. And that was the thing Kam loved about Scarlett, that she was always so willing to forgive or try to see the bright side.

Oh shit. Love.

Kam gulped and promised to review that emotion at a later date. "I think the panini has definitely given me some time to think about how I want to be treated by others. Life is too short to put up with a person that makes fun of you or your art."

Or Scarlett's perfect ass, but that seemed like it was better left unsaid, even if it was true.

"Yeah," Scarlet replied slowly. "Definitely something to think about."

"For sure." Kam tried to give Scarlett a smile, but it was slow and probably just as pained as it felt. She noticed Scarlett staring at her lip. "What?"

"You've got a little something," Scarlett said, and she reached out with one of her soft, clever fingers that Kam always admired, but she hesitated, hovering just over Kam's lower lip. "This okay?"

In a world where people tried to forget a pandemic, it was delightful to be asked for consent to touch.

"Absolutely."

And the soft pad of Scarlett's finger wiped whatever it was away from Kam's mouth, lingering at the corner like she was going to continue up and brush Kam's cheek. They lingered for a moment, the air heavy between them, and Scarlett's lips parted.

"Babe!"

Scarlett's eyes went wide and she sucked in a gasp. "Coming! Sorry, Kam, see you later."

"Good talk," Kam muttered to herself. She dumped out her cereal and went back to her room. Suddenly, she just wasn't in the mood for luck or charms.

It took a while, but eventually Kam talked herself into leaving the apartment. The stifling feeling had lingered too long, so she donned her mask and headed out for the nearest coffee shop, Devil's Stomping Grounds. Her thighs chafed as she walked, with her ragged cut-offs both riding up and getting a bit damp as she sweated in the summer sun, but it felt like a penance. Thou shalt not covet thy straight roommate, or some shit.

Eve had started Devil's Grounds a long time ago, maybe even decades, and she left the day to day operations to Quita and a handful of part-timers. It was a bastion of safety, really, where the local gays gathered. It was situated on main street, but it was angled into a courtyard that was shared with Vane Attraction Salon and Gallery QC. Through the pandemic, they'd put a whole bunch of rickety tables outside so people could still congregate, even if they probably shouldn't. It was too hot but everyone had been cooped up in their homes for so long they were willing to risk heat stroke if it meant getting outside.

"Kam! Haven't seen you in a while," Quita called happily. Her eyes crinkled up, showing she was smiling even though her face was covered. Her long braids were swept up today and tied up in a scarf that had a very familiar floral print to it. She was seated outside at one of the tables with a book in her hands. How she could stand to be out in the sun reading on a day like this was inconceivable.

"Hey! I love your scarf. Did Scarlett make you that?" Kam asked..

"Yeah, she did. Made the mask, too," Quita replied. Her eyes crinkled with a smile again.

"I thought that fabric looked familiar," Kam said. She gestured to the inside. "You're not working? On a Saturday morning?"

Quita rolled her eyes. "Eve has me on the closing shift tonight, so I'm just hanging out. Jesse should be stopping by soon."

"Awesome! Let me grab a drink and I'll come back, if that's okay," Kam said. She went to stand in line while Eve, who was training the new girl, made her a large iced vanilla latte. She took a croissant as well, just in case her appetite ever returned. Just a few weeks earlier, the card reader had been on a long stick that Quita or Eve would hold out to prevent any contact, but those days were fading as the usual tablet set-up returned. Kam's heart flipped a little, wondering if, maybe, everything was moving a bit too fast. It occurred to her that Kyle wasn't the only threat to her warm bubble of Scarlett. They'd be back to the office soon. Was it screwed up that she was enjoying this time a little? Even if it meant horrible things for other people?

"You okay?" Quita asked, watching Kam slump into the seat across from her. The sun was beating down on Kam's neck and making her sweat under her mask.

"Spare me from a minor in psych," Kam teased. She sighed, unable to help herself. "Do you ever think we're going too fast? I just, I dunno. Feels like everything is changing."

"Of course it is." Quita said. "Speaking of change, just a heads up that Jesse is going by he/him pronouns now."

Kam's eyes widened, and she chewed her straw. "Really? I'll keep that in mind. How do you feel about that?"

Everyone knew Quita's nesting partner, Jessie (now Jesse). Jessie lurked around Devil's Grounds most nights that Quita was working and talked to anyone that would stand still long enough about his love of theater. That was the thing- Jesse was an actor, and did a lot of the local community productions, but often complained about how hard it was to be a queer person in the theater scene. Coming out as trans was a big decision in such a small community.

Quita paused for a second with a pensive expression on her face. It caused her brows to knit and the skin around her eyes to crease. "Well, that's the thing about change. Maybe Jesse's pronouns are different, but that's still my Jesse. Jesse isn't different."

Kam nodded. "Good point."

Quita winked. "I'm always right."

"Kam!"

Oh, shit.

Kyle and Scarlett were headed their way, with Scarlett practically dragging Kyle along. They were unmasked, which was technically allowed outside but it felt like seeing them naked. Kam was almost sure, but not quite, that she heard him mutter a complaint about this specific coffee shop under his breath. A glance at Quita's face told her that Quita heard it, too, because the angry flash in her brown eyes and the furrow of her brows was an angry mirror of Kam's own expression. It was one thing to be a dickbean in private, but to act like a complete cock here, at Devil's, was completely unforgivable.

"Hey, Quita! Where's Jesse?" Scarlett asked. Kyle slid his hand in Scarlett's back pocket, using her jeans to pull her close to him. Kam wanted to choke. Or choke him. Either one.

"He's getting his hair cut," Quita said. She motioned across the little courtyard to Vane Attraction, a queer-friendly salon run by a really hot but really intimidating bisexual. Scarlett's eyes brightened.

"He? Well, that's exciting," Scarlett said. "Oh, cool, does that mean I can try making boy clothes?"

"He would love that," Quita told her and she squealed with delight. Kyle whined.

"Babe, why don't you ever make me boy clothes?" he said in a sing-songy voice.

"I thought you said you didn't want any when I asked you," Scarlett asked, confused.

Kyle stuttered, but then flashed Quita and Kam what he obviously thought was a charming smile. "I'd love it if you made me something."

Jesse was coming out of the salon just then, waving goodbye to the owner, Samantha Vane, as he stepped down into the courtyard. Before, when he'd been auditioning for female roles, he'd let his hair get super long. Now, Vane had buzzed off all the dark curls on the side, leaving a little poof on top that were still damp and tousled from being styled. He was wearing a bright pink button-up and a pair of well-fitting jeans, and he looked confident. More so than the last time Kam had seen him. She whistled.

Kyle choked on a laugh.

It was a really small laugh, but it was still a laugh and Jesse's happiness faded slightly, his face turning sour. "Got something to say, man?"

"Nah, bro, not at all," Kyle replied, but his returning smile wasn't nice. It was mean. Kam glanced at Scarlett and she was looking green around the edges.

"Looking good, Jesse. Hey, we gotta get back to the apartment. Scarlett has that big order for the Gallery to finish," Kam said hurriedly. She stood, and then gave into the impulse to reach over and squeeze Jesse's hand. "You look fucking amazing."

"You look gorgeous, babe," Quita said. Jesse quirked a brow at Kyle, who just snorted and tried to hide a giggle.

"See you guys later," Scarlett said. Her face was murderous, and she started to pull Kyle away. Kam just offered Quita a shrug.

"I fucking hate him."

"I don't know why you would," Jesse muttered. "Seems like a real winner."

"If that's true, I've never been so glad to have bad taste in all my life," Kam replied. She tipped her drink at the two of them. "See ya."

CHAPTER THREE

Another afternoon of staring at the ceiling and listening to the lovebirds bicker, Kam thought bitterly.

She couldn't quite make out what they were saying, but the walls hadn't grown any thicker so the tone of the words was definitely coming through loud and clear. Although, despite Scarlett's best shushing efforts, they were getting increasingly louder so Kam was probably going to hear some of it. She'd probably be able to hear all of it if she just pressed her ear against the door like a normal nosy person. But no, she was laying on her back on her bed, listening to the two of them argue, wishing she was doing literally anything else. Maybe she should put in some earbuds? Give them some privacy?

Kam wondered when everything had become earbuds. Instinctively, she still called them headphones, because that's what they'd been when she was younger.

Kam's family had been loud and she'd used her tape player and the headphones that came with it, purchased at the local dollar store for five bucks, to drown out the noise. The Best of the 60's girl band tape her grandma had gotten for free at the gas station was worn to nothing by the time tape players moved out and CD players were all the rage. Whether it had been loving or fighting, Kam's family had been a *lot* of drama and they'd never quite learned to regulate their voices to an 'inside' volume. Her body still tensed when there was a lot of shouting, and she instinctively wanted to crawl under the bed and hide. She'd spent a lot of afternoons down there, headphones on, devouring books while her brothers had played too loud or her parents fought (and consequently, made up).

So she was used to having to wait out a fight.

"Babe! I don't even see what the big damn deal is!"

Kyle's voice always made Kam a little uncomfortable, though. It was the vocal man-spread of it. The way that he ignored that this wasn't his house to boom and bellow, whether happy or sad or hungry, and it always caused her stomach to flip.

"The big deal is you ruined something I was working on! Something that mattered to me, and you don't understand why that's a problem!"

"Why are you even mad? It's just an ugly dress."

Kam sat up and slid off her bed, her bare feet barely making a noise as she crept towards the door. Maybe a little eavesdropping would be okay, after all. What the fuck did he do?

"They're not ugly!" Scarlett said angrily. Kyle made that weird ch-ing noise in the back of his throat. That guttural, dismissive not-quite-a-laugh that people made when they were being patronizing.

"I guess beauty is in the eye of the beholder. They're muumuus! Made out of old bed sheets! They're the ugliest thing I've ever seen," Kyle snapped. "It's so embarrassing to be seen with you, you know that?"

Kam's fingers clawed down the door as her blood started to simmer. What the actual fuck was he talking about? Scarlett looked adorable in her dresses. And she was so happy making them!

"Kyle, someone bought this from me. You ruined an order for a client-"

"Scarlett, wake up. You're not going to be a fashion designer making old curtains into shapeless tents!" Kyle bellowed.

Kam was about to wrench the door open and yell at him, but Scarlett was already biting back with,

"Are you going to be some big gamer? You gonna make a million dollars playing some gross apocalypse wet dream with all your gamer bros while you ignore the actual problems happening in the world?" Scarlett's voice was thick and wobbly in that way that said she was about to cry angry tears.

"Not if the fucking threads and dust from your fabric hoard and your stupid hobby is messing up my computers. And! I pulled a pin out of the blankets last night, so maybe I'm just doing you a favor since you can't be trusted to look after yourself," Kyle sneered. Kameron's nostrils flared.

"Get out, Kyle. I don't want to talk to you anymore," Scarlett snapped. "Take your computer and go home to your parents. I have rent to make and you've just set me back."

Kam cheered inside, but this wasn't the first time they'd had a big fight. Kyle would probably be gone a week and then he'd be right back to hogging the couch and eating all their food. Still, what a blessedly silent week it would be.

"The fuck, Scarlett?"

"You heard me! Get out!"

"Why? So you can make kissy faces at your dyke roommate? Ohhh, Kameron-"

Kam's blood was sizzling in her veins as she wrenched the door open. By the look on both their faces, neither of them expected her to be standing so close. Scarlett's door had been open, and Kam could see Kyle looming over her with his arms crossed over his chest, like he was trying to intimidate her with the fact that he was so much bigger than her. Kam had two seconds to take in the sight before her, for Kyle to see the murderous expression on her face, before Scarlett spoke in a low, commanding voice.

"Get out, Kyle."

His mouth opened like he was going to continue to argue with her, but with the pair of women glaring at him, he conceded defeat for the moment. He started stuffing things in his bag - all his gaming toys, his headphones and laptop, and then he went for the front door. When he brushed past Scarlett, Kam was sure he knocked her with his arm on purpose. Scarlett just stared after him in an angry silence. Kam wondered if she should close the door again and give them more privacy, but she also didn't want to leave her roommate alone with this douchecanoe.

"I'll call you," Kyle said as he headed for the door, and it sounded like a threat.

"Don't bother," Scarlett shot back. The front door made a loud slam as he closed it behind him and then they were finally alone. Which was good, because Scarlett was going to pieces. She flung herself towards Kameron, and Kam wrapped her up in the tightest hug she could manage and rocked her as she cried.

"It's okay, honey. It's okay," Kam murmured. The 'honey' just slipped out, and Kam blushed over it, but Scarlett didn't seem to notice.

"He sabotaged my machine!" Scarlet complained as she cried. "I knew he didn't like my sewing, but to just mess it up like that, and I can't get it to work and- and he ripped a hole in one of the sleeves-"

"We'll work it out. We'll figure out a way to get it fixed, okay?" Kam asked. She pulled back so she could look at Scarlett's face, which was flushed and warm. She wiped the tears from Scarlett's cheeks. "It's going to work out."

"It's just- I would- I would never," Scarlett choked. "And he just laughed like it was nothing." She leaned back forward, burying her face against Kam's shoulder. The way she squeezed Kam so tight, the way it felt, was incredible. Which Kam felt immediately guilty about. But God, their bodies fit together really nicely.

"I know, you're a good partner to him. Look, it's still early. Maybe that place on Fourth Street is still open," Kam said, swallowing hard as the scent of Scarlett's hair filled her nose. "You go pack up Ruby and I'll give them a call, okay?"

"Okay," Scarlett managed. She gave Kam a watery smile. "I can't work on my stuff tonight."

"That's okay. I think we need a movie night, anyway. I have a massive deficiency in vitamin popcorn," Kam teased. She shoved her hands in her pockets and shrugged her shoulders upwards. "Maybe we could watch that Marilyn movie you've been trying to show me. The gay one."

"God, Marilyn is so…" Scarlett scrunched up her face as she trailed off, and Kam couldn't have been more smitten.

So are you, Kam thought.

"It was my queer awakening," Scarlett continued as she bent to unplug the sewing machine from the wall outlet. Kam's brows knit together. That was new. They'd lived together for a while now, through a whole pandemic, and she had no idea Scarlett was anything other than straight. "Jack Lemmon's character and his little old loverboy is my favorite part."

"Okay, so, here's what we do. You pack up Ruby, I'll call the repair people," Kam said, as she needed to remind herself of exactly what she was supposed to be doing instead of watching Scarlett's fine ass in those handmade jeans. "And then we'll stop over at Devil's to get some coffee. Then we'll come back here, get in our PJ's and watch movies all night. Maybe we'll even get plastered."

"Cuddle puddle on your bed?" Scarlett asked, turning her wide, pleading eyes on Kam. Kam grinned.

"Of course."

According to the repair place, Ruby would not be ready until later in the week. Scarlett's feet dragged as they walked back towards Devil's Stomping Grounds. Quita was on shift by then and she leaned over the counter to whisper at Kam, "Yo, what's wrong with your girlfriend?"

"She's not my girlfriend," Kam mumbled back through her mask. She glanced over her shoulder at Scarlett, sitting down at one of the tables, looking dejected. Her eyes were still puffy from crying and red around the edges. "I think she broke up with her boyfriend."

"Okay," Quita said, dragging the word out until it had about three extra syllables. "So, what's wrong with your future girlfriend?"

"Shh! Don't let her hear you say that," Kam snapped quietly. Quita pursed her lips and gave Kam a look that definitely showed which, of the two of them, would win in a fight.

"Look, that guy was a fucking asshole today," Quita said as she began to pull the drinks. She filled the to-go cups full of ice and Kam had a momentary hope of Quita launching at her to cool her down. No such luck.

"He was, but that doesn't mean she's going to be my girlfriend," Kameron said. Quita frowned.

"Why not?"

"Because. It just, it doesn't," Kameron replied. Quita rolled her eyes.

"Look, I'm not the relationship advice person, but I can tell you, don't wait. Sometimes these asshole guys, they can be sticky like simple syrup and it's easy to get sucked back in." Quita took Kameron's money from her. "I don't want to give him a chance to get his mitts back into her. You, I don't give a fuck about you."

"Shut up!" Kameron said with a laugh. Quita smiled.

"But her, she deserves the sweet care that's written all over your face every time you're near her," Quita said.

"Sounds suspiciously like relationship advice," Kameron commented and Quita almost threw a napkin at her.

"Maybe I'll ask her out and you'll all be sorry!"

Kameron laughed but then she straightened and looked afraid. "No! Don't. Please don't."

Quita gave her a secretive smile. "Guess you better get on it, then."

It was too hot and humid to sit outside, so Scarlett had found one of the most socially distanced tables in the back of the cafe. She was curled towards the wall, but she smiled when Kam approached.

"Here you go," Kameron said, handing Scarlett her iced americano.

"Thanks," she murmured. "You're a good friend, Kameron."

Kam's lips twitched as she replied, "Thanks. I try."

"Well, you succeed," Scarlett said. She was too pink, and her forehead was a little damp, but Kam assumed it was from walking back on such a warm afternoon. Kam reached down to grab her hand and pulled her to her feet.

"Come on, let's go get the cuddle puddle started. I can already taste the popcorn," Kam said. Scarlett winced, but she didn't let go of Kam's hand.

"We'll have to stop at the store. I think Kyle might have eaten yours," Scarlett told her.

Kam rolled her eyes. Of fucking course he did.

CHAPTER FOUR

Jack Lemmon was on a boat in the middle of the ocean and he was objecting to his lover's proposal loudly enough that it woke Kameron. She inhaled through her nose, her eyes squinting at the laptop screen, and gave a little grunt. Osgood had proposed to his girlfriend, who turned out to be a man, and in the most iconic proposal of movie history, he'd just accepted it. No one is perfect, Kam thought to herself as Jack just smiled blithely. They were literally riding off into the sunset and it warmed Kam from the inside out. Love didn't have to be that hard. It could just be.

"I'm glad he got a happy ending," Kam said out loud, her voice rough with sleep. There was no reply, but maybe Scarlett was just as bleary as she was. As the credits rolled, she realized she was warm, and her limbs were weighted down by something heavier than a blanket. Pinned in place, she glanced down.

So maybe Scarlett was asleep.

On Kam.

Somewhere during the film, Scarlett had nuzzled close, practically burrowing her face in Kam's neck. Her red hair was everywhere, reminding Kam of a mermaid under the ocean, fluffing out in a messy cloud. A possessive arm cuddled Kam like a teddy bear, pulling her so their bodies were slotted together. Kam's arm was wrapped around Scarlett's waist, and she grinned as she tugged the other girl closer. She reached over to her nightstand to grab her phone, lifting it up so she could take a selfie. She wondered if she should feel guilty, but if she forwarded a copy to Scarlett, too, it wouldn't be weird, right?

Scarlett's phone buzzed from somewhere in the room as Kam forwarded her a copy of the pick. Hopefully that didn't make it weirder. But she just looked so cute!

She probably should have woken Scarlett up instead of taking pictures of her like a weirdo, but she was warm and sleepy, and she just couldn't bring herself to care. She put her phone down, let out a long breath and wrapped her arm tighter around Scarlett. Curled up in their warm little nest, Kam drifted back to sleep feeling something just next to happy.

Kam woke up to several things happening all at once.

The first thing was the shouting. There was a loud, angry voice screaming from somewhere in the building. It was muffled, but it was loud, and it was calling Scarlett's name.

Oh, for fuck's sake, Kyle, have some dignity.

The second thing, which Kam wished she could have registered as the first thing but Kyle was taking up too much space, as usual, was that she was alone in bed. Her fingers reached out to grip the sheets where Scarlett had been curled. She could smell the familiar shampoo scent lingering on her pillow. That wasn't weird, right? That she knew Scarlett's shampoo? She'd had to borrow it once or twice when she'd run out, although she tried not to because what was formulated for Scarlett's thick, curling strands did not work on Kam's fine, stringy mess. It always made her too greasy.

Kyle's fists pounded on the front door, bringing Kam's scattered thoughts back to the first thing. What number of things were they up to? Oh, number three.

The third thing Kam became aware of was the distinct smell of burnt breakfast in the air.

Oh, *shit*, Scarlett couldn't cook to save her life.

Kam's feet hit the rug and she was out of her bedroom door as quick as she could move, leaving the warm sheets and soft scents for later reflection.

"Scarlett! Get your ass out here and explain yourself!"

Give it the fuck up, Kyle. You lost, Kameron thought, as she went towards the kitchen. It was a disaster, but nothing was on fire this time, so Kam wouldn't have to call Mr. Tsui and explain why the couple downstairs was upset about the smoke. There was an open egg carton on the counter, half filled with empty shells and half with whole eggs. There was flour on all of the counters and some of the floor. There was coffee, thank God, and the stack of pancakes that was on one of their cheap china plates didn't look too bad. The bacon, though. That was a lost cause.

"Oh! Kam! You're awake!" Scarlett said, whirling to give Kam a mildly manic smile. Kam's brows knit together.

"Yeah. You okay?" Kam crossed her arms over her chest, her heart racing as the thumping on their door continued. "Something you want to talk about?"

"Okay so like, promise you won't be mad," Scarlett said as she turned back to the stove to flip the last pancake. "I just wanted to do something nice for you, so I thought I'd make you breakfast! You know, because you've been so nice to me. I thought we could eat and maybe walk down to the farmer's market or something, you know, because you like to support local businesses-"

"Scarlett," Kam said, her low tone almost a warning.

"Okay, so I also might have posted that picture of the two of us to the 'grams, okay? I know, it was rotten and I shouldn't have done it without asking you first but it was just so cute and my followers know that you're helping me out and I thought they'd eat it right up," Scarlett said, her words a fast jumble as she spoke. She turned off the burner and faced Kam again. God, there was flour in her hair and on her nose. Kam licked her lips.

"Great, so your followers saw a picture of us..." Kam's brain finally caught up. "Oh."

"Yes. Oh."

"Kyle also saw?" Kam guessed. She guessed correctly if the guilty expression crossing Scarlett's face was anything to go off of.

"Sort of? Yes. And he's mad."

"Are you two..." Kam winced as Kyle called Scarlett's name again. "Are you two thinking of getting back together?"

"Fuck no," Scarlett said quickly. "Could you imagine? It's just, he's here now and I want him to leave, so I've just been ignoring him."

"Scarlett! I can hear you!"

"I can hear you, too, you jackass! I will call the cops on you!" Kameron shouted back, her eyes never leaving Scarlett's pained expression. She raised her eyebrow. "You were saying?"

"Well, it was a really cute picture. I really liked it," Scarlett explained. "So I might have posted it on my socials. A bit. Okay, like on every account."

Kameron's jaw dropped. "Everywhere? Even..?"

Scarlett nodded. "Even there. I just decided, you know, some things are worth it and I really, really loved the picture. And everything we did, really. I- I should've asked, I know, but I thought if he thought I moved on, maybe he'd stop DMing me, too-"

Kameron's heart sank. Of course Scarlett only posted because she wanted Kyle to leave her alone. And guys like Kyle wouldn't take something like their ex-girlfriend entering a queer relationship well. *Step away now, Kameron.* Let Scarlett be a big girl and clean up her own damn messes.

"We are going to need to have a super long talk about this," Kameron said. But the pounding was persistent. "But first, what are we going to do about him?"

"You could call the cops. We've asked him to leave us alone and he's still going at it," Scarlett suggested.

"You, You could call the cops," Kameron replied. Scarlett nodded.

"I meant that. I'm sorry, Kameron, I really don't want to put you in a place where you're fixing problems for me, it's just we're here together and I guess I dragged you into this. I'm so sorry. I don't want you to be in the middle," Scarlett said.

"Well, I'm in the middle now, Scarlett," Kameron said.

"Scarlett!"

"Oh, fuck this shit," Kam growled and she stepped over to yank the door open. She glared at the man in question, making sure to blink up at him innocently. "What's up, Kyle?"

"Move out of the way, I want to talk to Scarlett," Kyle demanded, and he started to push forward.

"She's calling the cops. Just like I said she would, and then she's calling our landlord and we're filing so many reports against you, including a restraining order," Kameron told him. She angled the door again, trying to keep him out, and used her full body to block the narrow space she allowed herself to look out of. Scarlett came to stand next to her, nibbling on her nails, but helping act as a door stop so he couldn't push his way inside the apartment.

Kyle fumed. Kam hadn't noticed until this very moment how much like a bull he looked. His nostrils were flared out, and his eyes were wide with anger. "I told you to get out of my way."

"And I've told you to get out of my apartment. A lot. So, maybe do that?" Kam suggested in a cheery, helpful tone. She risked a glance at Scarlett, who pretended to be on the phone.

"Hello? Yes?" Scarlett said. "Um, I'd like to report someone trespassing and threatening my girlfriend."

Kameron tried her very best to ignore the word girlfriend. Remember, Kam, it was all part of the show. She looked back to Kyle, letting her lips curve into a smug smile. "See? She's calling the cops."

"In Quaint City?" Kyle sneered. He dropped his arms to cross them over his chest, apparently having decided that it was his turn to look smug. "Yeah. Sure. The cops here don't really care about queers."

"Maybe the cops you talk to haven't," Kam said. It was kind of sad because she knew that he wasn't wrong. In an emergency, she probably wouldn't rely on some of the townies in QC to come to her defense, but she was willing to believe that he would go without too much of an argument.

"Yeah, he's banging down our door and he won't leave," Scarlett said as she attempted to continue pretending with her conversation. "How quickly can you be here? We're really worried he's going to harm himself or someone else."

"Scarlett! That's some bullshit!" Kyle said. His fist reached out and slammed the door again. If it hadn't been for both of their bodies holding fast, he probably would have managed to bust in, but they managed to keep him out. Sadly, Scarlett's head got knocked against the wood in the process.

"Kyle, I'd go if I were you. Before you have to appear in court," Kam said. She picked up her foot and stamped hard on his. She knew it wasn't hard enough to break his toes, but a girl could wish.

Kyle seemed to consider this. From what Kam knew, Kyle's family wasn't broke, but they also weren't supportive enough of their son to bail him out of jail if the cops were called, as evidenced by the fact that he'd spent all summer on their sofa, eating their food, while also keeping a room with his parents. If he was arrested, would he have anyone to bail him out? Probably not.

"There's someone on their way?" Scarlet asked. "Thank you, officer!"

"Whatever. You're not even fucking worth it," Kyle sneered. "Cowards."

Well, that stung just a little. They were not cowards. But Kam was willing to let that slide in the hopes that the peace would be restored soon.

"Bye, bruh," Kam said, and as soon as Kyle had cleared the door, she slammed it shut and flipped the locks. All of them. With a heavy sigh, she leaned forward, so her forehead was touching the wooden panel and she sighed again for good measure.

"Thank you," Scarlett said softly.

"I can't believe he fell for that," Kam replied. She let her eyes close for a long moment, processing the stress of the last few minutes.

"Well, he's not super bright," Scarlett pointed out.

Anger and hurt flared in Kameron's chest. She closed her eyes, the wood still pressing into her skin. "Why? Why did you post the picture? You had to know he was going to do something like that."

"It was a cute picture," Scarlett said with a shrug.

Kameron straightened. "But you had to know, Scarlett. People are going to think we're a couple. Kyle thinks we're a couple. You said-"

Girlfriend. Scarlett had called her 'girlfriend'.

Scarlett squirmed uncomfortably. "It's still a cute picture. We look happy."

And she had Kameron there. They did look happy. Scarlett looked utterly peaceful, curled against Kameron, gripping her like a favorite stuffed animal. Kameron looked sleepy and content. It was a good picture.

"Why did you take the picture?" Scarlett asked softly. "If you didn't want anyone to see it."

Well, that was the rub of it. Kameron couldn't very well criticize Scarlett if Kameron was also vaguely guilty of not admitting her own feelings. Kameron managed a shrug. "I don't know."

"Okay. So I'm sorry for posting it to social media without your consent. Are you sorry for taking a picture of me without asking first?" Scarlett asked, and her voice was so gentle. Kameron blushed.

"Yeah. I'm sorry," she said.

"Awesome. We're both sorry," Scarlett said with a shrug. She took Kameron's hand and pulled her towards the kitchen. "The rest of it, we can work that out later when we've calmed down. Look! I made pancakes!"

And Kameron was going to eat them, even if they looked like roof shingles.

CHAPTER FIVE

"So, you..." Kam bit her lip and tucked some of her hair behind her ear as it escaped her ponytail. The summer sun was beating down on her again and, as sweaty as she felt, it wasn't uncomfortable today. Today she was walking too close to a sexy girl who had spent the entire night in her arms, and who had cooked her breakfast. An adorable (if burnt) breakfast. So adorable that it was probably going to drive Kam up a wall if this went on too much longer.

Kam tried again. "So you said that Marilyn was your queer awakening. How long have you known? I mean, I feel like I've known you forever and I had no idea that you were-"

"Bi? Oh yeah, I think I've always known," Scarlett replied. They were at the farmer's market, perusing the jams and jellies offered by locals. She stopped at one booth to pick up a jar of honey that cost more than what Kam made in a day, turning it over in her hands. Kam was patently not thinking about licking it off of her naked body. "I'm lucky, I guess. I never had to question it. It just... is. It's how it's always been."

"Ah," Kam managed. "You just seem so..."

"Straight?" Scarlett laughed, and she put the sexy honey down. "You're kidding, right? My curtains are literally the bi flag."

Kam thought back to the pattern on Scarlett's curtains, and her eyes widened. "Oh. Oh my God."

Scarlett laughed again. "You think someone who dresses like a cosplayer of Miss Frizzle could possibly be straight? Sweetie, are you serious?"

Okay, point taken. The next booth was individual charcuterie cups and mini wine bottles, which sounded like a fantastic idea because dairy and alcohol on a hot morning in August would be the perfect treat. Kam paid for both of them and Scarlett spotted a shady bench under a tree on the other side of the park. As they headed there, a voice called out from one of the food trucks,

"Traitors!"

Kam turned to smile at Max, a friend of hers who was hanging out of their food truck and waving. She waved back, but kept moving.

"You know them?" Scarlett asked.

"Oh, yeah, they used to come to Devil's all the time. The truck was supposed to be run by them and their childhood best friend, but Cordie needed time off when, you know, the world exploded," Kam said with a sigh. She sat down on the bench next to Scarlett and picked up a skewer of grapes from her cup. "I think Max was a little in love with Cordie, but it would never have worked out. I'm not even sure how they're running the truck alone."

"Why wouldn't it have worked out?" Scarlett asked, smearing some half-melted brie onto a piece of toast. Kam shrugged.

"They were really, really good friends, and you're not supposed to go into partnerships with your friends, right? Everything is too personal. Cordie and Max bickered a lot," Kam replied. She wondered if that was telling. You know, don't go into business with friends, don't go into relationships with roommates. Either way someone was going to get hurt.

"Sounds like it was trouble before they added in the truck," Scarlett replied. She lifted her tiny rosé to her lips to take a drink. "Is that something that worries you? Like, worrying you're going to start something with someone and then they leave?"

Kam shrugged. "I don't know. The women I've been with have all started out as strangers. I've never fallen for a friend before."

"Never?"

Scarlett's eyes were wide and dewy when Kam turned to look at her. Big mistake. Those eyes could have gotten Kam to do anything in that exact moment.

"Well," Kam whispered. "Almost never."

They both blushed and then returned to stuffing salami into their mouths, which should have been a choking hazard with how hilarious that irony was. They were quiet. From their shaded park bench, Kam could see Max whirling around in their truck, attempting to take orders and fill them all at the same time. They looked tired, but happy.

"You never told me what your gay awakening was," Scarlett said, after a few minutes.

"It took me a while. And I don't know that I had one, really. I was obsessed with this stupid boy band, Plum Drum Cult, and I really had a thing for their lead singer," Kam told her. Scarlett giggled.

"Oh, I cannot even imagine you liking Reggie from P.D.C.," Scarlett giggled. Kam chuckled and nodded.

"I was obsessed. I had their posters on my wall, and I thought, gosh I couldn't possibly be gay, I love this band," Kam said. She swallowed hard. "But, the thing with boy bands in the nineties was that they were all kind of... well. Feminine, in retrospect."

Scarlett started to giggle again. "Is that why you moved here? Because you know Reggie is from Quaint City?"

Kam snorted. "No! Not at all."

"Oh em gee, you totally moved here to stalk a boy band," Scarlett teased, and Kam couldn't stop laughing.

"I did not!"

"Definitely did. Creep," Scarlett said, and her giggles softened. "Did you ever have a bowl cut?"

"Look, the things that happened in the nineties stay in the nineties. Unless, you know. You ask my mom really nice at Christmas. She just loves to whip out those photo albums," Kam said, biting her pickle rather enthusiastically. Scarlett grinned and reached over to steal one of Kam's grapes.

"I'll have to remember that," Scarlett said quietly and Kam was definitely not going to get excited about the idea of spending Christmas with Scarlett.

Ok, maybe she would a little.

It was a truth universally acknowledged that Monday mornings were significantly improved by the absence of men named Kyle. Sunday had ended with blissful calm. There had been separate showers, which felt nice after being in the sun for so long, and cooking dinner with their freshly purchased farmers market veg. There'd been an impromptu photo shoot on the fire escape with some of the garments that Kyle didn't destroy and then Scarlett had messed around with editing them for her social media accounts, so Kam picked up a novel she'd been reading during more peaceful apartment times and sprawled out on their couch. It felt decadent, knowing that no one was going to stomp through or shout. They parted ways at bedtime in the most awkward way Kam had ever said goodnight to anyone. It had looked, for a moment, like Scarlett was going to lean in, but neither of them had done that and both of them looked like they regretted it.

Kam slept until almost time for her fourth alarm to go off, and she rolled out of bed and glanced in a mirror just long enough to pull a brush through her hair. She sat down at her tiny desk, flipped open her laptop and began signing into the apps that she used for work.

Around midmorning, while she was muted during the most boring company training meeting yet, her door creaked open and Scarlett appeared. She was holding Kam's favorite mug. It was a white ceramic mug with a red lid that made it look like a mushroom. Scarlett had bought it for her after it went viral online.

"Thank you," Kam breathed with a smile as Scarlett handed the cup to her. A label confirming that this was a cup of Kam's favorite tea fluttered from a string on the side. Scarlett smiled back.

"You didn't come out for coffee earlier. I thought you could use a boost," Scarlett whispered with a wink before leaving the room and closing the door. The video call chat lit up with the intrigue of Kameron's mystery tea maker.

Majd: (10:34 AM) Oh my Gosh is that your roommate?

John: (10:35 AM) Are you dating?

John: (10:36 AM) I thought you were single…

Majd: (10:38 AM) She's adorable. Where did she get that top?

Truthfully, Kam hadn't noticed Scarlett's clothes today. She'd been too busy being intoxicated with the warm smile and happy light that had been in Scarlett's eyes. Scarlett hadn't looked that comfortable in her own skin in a long time.

Kam: (10:40 AM) Just a friend.

David: (10:41 AM) Keep this chat professional, guys. Pay attention to the speaker.

John: (10:42 AM) Yes, boss.

Majd: (10:42 AM) I wish my husband would bring me tea.

John: (10:43 AM) Wait does it count as uhauling if they already live together?

Kam giggled and closed the chat so she could continue listening to the lecture. She couldn't help but feel flattered that Scarlett had come looking for her. She'd never brought Kam tea before. So, at Kameron's lunch break, she went into the kitchen and threw together a couple of sandwiches. There were still some essentials that they needed to replenish after the Kyle situation, but their trip to the market had given them… okay, a bare minimum of things to work with. Still, she took the little sandwich on a cute plate into Scarlett's room.

Scarlett was sitting with her laptop on her bed on a wooden tray she'd gotten at a vintage shop pre-pandemic. One of those old breakfast tray situations. She had on flannel moon-phase pajama bottoms, but her top was an adorable printed blouse that gave her a professional appearance from the waist-up. Kam grinned. Peak Scarlett. That whole, "I'm only going to do the bare minimum to please you because professional clothing is boring and uncomfortable."

Scarlett muted her screen and gave Kam a slow, delighted smile. "Thanks. I was getting pretty hangry."

"No worries. You need anything else?" Kam asked, unable to stop her own mouth from spreading into a grin.

"Water? Sorry, I just-"

"No, of course. No problem. I'll be right back," Kam said, waving off her protests. Of course, she should've thought to bring a drink. She snuck back in and placed a glass of ice water next to Scarlett, winking at her as the meeting droned on through the speakers.

Just as she started to leave, Scarlett muted again and said, "So I was thinking, if you wanted, we could watch another movie tonight. You know, I can't do any sewing with my machine still in the shop."

Kam's eyebrows rose. "You sure?"

"Yeah! Of course!" Scarlett nodded enthusiastically. "We could spread out dinner on the coffee table and watch it on the TV, you know, since *he's* not here anymore to interrupt us."

Kam's smile widened. "That would be awesome."

Scarlett scrunched her nose. "Awesome. It's a date."

CHAPTER SIX

By the end of the day, neither of them felt much like cooking. Even ramen seemed to be just a little bit beyond what either of them had the mental capacity for. In such a short amount of time, everything had started to shift between them, and it was a lot to process.

"I don't know what to get, though," Scarlett complained. She'd changed out of her work shirt and into a pink ribbed tank that matched the little moons on her pajama bottoms. Rather than clashing with her red hair, it highlighted how rosy her skin was, clinging to her curves in a way Kam could grow to appreciate. Her stomach growled. She was slumped in a kitchen chair with her head resting on the table in front of her, looking at Kam, who was sprawled out on the sofa. "All I know is that I don't want to get dressed but I'm starving."

"Okay, I saw this on the clock app," Kam said. She stood and grabbed her phone. "We can use a randomizer and pick what we want to eat."

"Oh, like a game?" Scarlett said. She sat up in her chair, grinning at Kam. "That sounds fun."

"Yeah, it'll be fun," Kam said. She slid into the chair across from Scarlett and opened her phone to one of the random wheel generator sites she'd seen. "Okay, so what about pizza?"

Scarlett frowned. "We just had pizza."

"I mean, that's true, but we need options on the wheel," Kam told her. She shrugged. "We don't have to pick pizza."

"Well," Scarlett hummed, and she tilted her head to the side as she considered. "Yeah, don't put pizza on the list. Indian food?"

Kam put the Indian restaurant on the list, despite the fact that they'd still have to leave the apartment to pick it up and it was actually on the outskirts of Quaint City, not downtown. "Gotcha. What about Chinese?"

"Definitely. Chili mac from the gas station doesn't sound bad," Scarlett said thoughtfully, and Kam grinned at her.

"Is that what you want?" Kam asked.

"No, I'm not saying that," Scarlett replied, and she leaned forward again but this time she rested her head on her arms, staring right at Kam as though she didn't want to look away. "I'm just saying if I had to eat something, I could probably get that and feel okay. What else?"

In the end, the picker wheel chose Chinese food, and Kam placed the order for it to be delivered. Which was really nice, because Kam definitely didn't feel like leaving the house. The bubble they'd created felt so delicate and pure that she just wanted to revel in it, worry about the next step later. She had this itching feeling like if she left, even to get food, something would break. Scarlett put on an old sitcom from the nineties and they spread out the white boxes of takeout on their coffee table. They sat side-by-side on the floor, with their backs against the couch and a fluffy blanket underneath them, and shared their food. They'd ordered too much, but that was okay because it would last them now that their garbage monster wasn't eating everything in sight.

"Kyle hated this show," Scarlett said around a mouthful of rice.

"Kyle hates fun," Kam told her. She slurped up her plain lo-mein noodles, ordered just as she had ever since she was a child and watched *The Lost Boys* for the first time. If David didn't need vegetables, then neither did Kam. She washed down the salty tang of soy sauce with the cheap beer she'd found at the bottom of the fridge. It wasn't like Kyle was coming back for it.

"That's so true," Scarlett replied.

"I'm surprised you like it, though. It seems like the kind of show you wouldn't really enjoy," Kam said before she could stop herself. Scarlett's brows furrowed, creating that sweet dimple between them and the one that appeared at the corner of her mouth whenever she frowned. "I mean, it's just kind of normal? And so straight. Like, it's definitely classic and all, but I just figured you'd pick something more... whimsical?"

"Ah," Scarlett said, and she bit her lip as she considered this. "We watched it a lot when I was a kid. My mom was obsessed, like, one of those fans who wanted to know which of the guys was the father and seriously set the timer each week to tune in. But it's also a good time capsule for clothes. I was talking to my autistic friend about stimming, and how she also looks for visual stims, and I think it might be one of my visual stims. I'm always looking at the outfits, deconstructing them in my mind, trying to take them apart and remake them. It's probably weird-"

"That's not weird at all," Kam said quickly, and she reached out to touch Scarlett's hand. "Not even a little."

Scarlett grinned at her. "Thank you. You're always so supportive of me."

"I think that everyone should be supported. Especially when they do such cool things, like creating," Kam told her softly. "Your ex... he just seemed to hate everything about you."

"That's very true," Scarlett agreed.

"Which sucks, because you're fucking amazing," Kam said before her mouth could stop her. Scarlett bumped into her, and Kam was painfully aware of how close they were. Their hips were pressed together, their arms touching. Scarlett's body was so soft against Kam's.

Kam thought back to the other night, when they were also soft and warm and pressed together, only in a more horizontal position.

She blushed, and took another sip from her can of beer. "Well. It's true. You're amazing, Scarlett."

So far, a lot of things had been true. Kyle was a giant douchecanoe? Yup. Scarlett deserved better? Check. Kam was painfully in love with Scarlett? Triple check!

"Kam?"

Kam froze, her heart beating quickly. Scarlett was still so close, with her eyes fixed on the swell of Kam's lower lip. She registered that she could hear Scarlett breathing, in and out, ragged and heavy. Kam's lashes fluttered. She wasn't used to Scarlett being the more forward of the two of them. Seeing the way she was leaning in, as if she was about to assert more control over the situation, was one of the sexiest things Kam had ever been given. It was like their own little secret.

"Scarlett?" Kam whispered. Scarlett's eyes flicked upward. Her pupils were blown out, her lids heavy and hazy.

"Is this okay, Kam?" Scarlett asked, but it almost wasn't a question, it was a statement. "Is this-" There was a hint of her typical uncertainty, those brows meeting briefly only to smooth again. "Is this what you want?"

"You. I've always wanted you," Kam managed quietly. Scarlett leaned in more, just a tiny bit, but enough.

"Tell me," Scarlett said, and her mouth was so close to Kam's.

"Yes, Scarlett. I want this," Kam said. She took Scarlett's hand at the same time Scarlett moved closer, closing the distance between them. Their lips crashed together in a furiously delicious kiss. Everything else, the forgotten food and the soft noise of the sitcom, faded to the background as the foreground became focused on the press of their lips together and the slide of their tongues. Quickly, they were figuring out how to untangle their limbs from their side-by-side position, and move. Down, down, backwards, to the side, until Kam was laying with her back on the fuzzy blanket and Scarlett was positioned over her.

"You are so beautiful," Scarlett breathed when they forced themselves to come up for air. She was propped up with one arm, but used her free hand to stroke down Kam's cheek, like she'd wanted to a few days earlier but hadn't been able to. She ducked down to kiss Kam again.

"You are," Kam argued, but she realized it wasn't a competition. They could both be utterly beautiful for each other.

"The way you look at me," Scarlett said, and she dipped down to kiss along Kam's jaw, leaving a fevered trail of sweet kisses and sharp nibbles. "When you take the pictures, when you're telling me I need to eat- it makes me feel seen. Taken care of. I love to watch you when you're watching me."

"It's easy to watch you," Kam admitted. "It's easy to care about you."

"Sometimes it hasn't seemed like it. For other people," Scarlett told her. She blew in Kameron's ear, causing her to shiver. "Is this okay?"

"Yeah," Kam said. Scarlett's hands found Kam's wrists and tugged them up, pinning her arms over her head. Scarlett looked down at Kam with nothing but heat and caring.

"Is it really?"

On the grand scale of things Kameron didn't know she wanted but turned out were the only thing she ever wanted, being pinned by Scarlett was number one. Now it was Kam's turn to breathe out in a ragged sigh, nodding furiously. "Yes. I want it."

"Tell me where else," Scarlett said, and she returned to Kam's ear to nip gently at the earlobe. "Where do you want me?"

"Everywhere," Kam admitted. Scarlett laughed, and she nipped at Kam's ear once more before beginning to work herself lower. Her lips trailed along the column of Kam's neck.

"Eventually," Scarlett said.

"M-My collar bone," Kam suggested, and her blush deepened. Scarlet licked over the hollow of Kam's neck before humming against her skin.

"Beautiful collar bones," Scarlett murmured, and she pressed her lips there, too. She opened her mouth, sucking inward, but not quite biting. She soothed the skin with her tongue. "Sweet, beautiful collar bones."

"What about you?" Kam asked and she tried to look down but all she was met with was a chaotic swirl of curls.

"No, sweetheart, this is for you," Scarlett said. "We'll do me after. Can I go lower?"

Kam gulped, and she didn't trust herself to do anything

more than nod. Scarlett's hand worked Kam's tee shirt up over her torso, and Kam lifted briefly to help her get it off. Scarlett's gaze was absolutely ravenous when she realized that Kam wasn't wearing a bra. Her tongue darted out, wetting her lips, and she bent to kiss Kam's mouth again. The soft cotton of Scarlett's ribbed tank top rubbed against Kam's bare skin, making her shiver.

"You are a gift," Scarlett said sweetly. She pulled back and continued her trail, kissing down the center of Kameron's body, between her breasts and then pulling one nipple into her mouth. She swirled, and sucked, until Kam was just on the verge of being too sensitive and then she switched. "Is this okay?"

Her tongue was making lazy circles around Kam's nipple, and then she blew on it which was almost too much.

"It's okay, but it's not my favorite," Kam admitted with a wince. "Is that cool?"

"Absolutely. Anything for you," Scarlett said. "But just so you know, mine are very sensitive. In case you want to return the favor later."

Kam definitely wanted to do that, so she nodded vigorously. Scarlett laughed and then traced her tongue down the curve of Kam's breast, pressing a kiss just under it. Her hands released Kam's, but not before a gentle, "Keep them up there, like a good girl, okay?"

Kam was pretty sure she wasn't going to come untouched, but the idea of Scarlett, sweet Scarlett who barely ever seemed to ask for anything, calling Kam a good girl was enough to consider the option.

"Okay."

"Beautiful," Scarlett said again. Perhaps it was the connoisseur in her that made her like this. Kam knew that Scarlett had an appreciation for the weird- like her dresses that she made- or for good food. She was someone who enjoyed savoring, and right now she was definitely savoring Kam. Her hands smoothed down over Kam's bare chest and then squeezed her hips. Kam, who hadn't been sensible enough to put on pajamas for easy access, was in jeans, but she suddenly didn't mind. Scarlett's clever crafty hands were pressing at her over her clothes. One hand pressed gently into the flesh over Kam's pelvic bone, the other stroking much lower.

Thank fucking God for the seams on a pair of jeans. The pressure was *incredible*.

"Scarlett," Kam whimpered. "Scar-"

"Is this okay? Are we still okay?" Scarlett asked, turning those wide eyes on Kam. Kam was unable to verbalize, only nod, that fuck *yes* they were okay. "Are you going to come for me like this, sweetheart? Can you come just like-"

Kam was aware how loud her breathing had gotten as she lost herself to the wave of Scarlett pressing, touching, separated from her skin by a layer of denim. The friction, the fact that it was Scarlett, it was all becoming too much. Especially since Scarlett leaned forward and started leaving even more kisses - a sucking one to the side of Kam's stomach, a sweet one between her breasts again, a loving one to the tip of her nipple, all while those capable hands pressed and rubbed and shook until Kam was the one shaking.

"Oh, oh my God, oh my God, Scarlett!" Kam exclaimed, unable to stop her eyes from closing as her orgasm rushed through her, causing her to shake apart in Scarlett's arms. She was sweating. When had she started to sweat?

"That's right, yes, yes, Kam," Scarlett said, holding her through it all. Her hands were replaced with her thigh, giving Kam a gentle pressure, but not too much to where she was overly sensitive.

"That was..." Kam managed. Scarlett's answering laugh was breathy and soft.

"You are so fucking beautiful," Scarlett told her.

"I love you," Kam said, and then she froze. She wasn't- she hadn't meant to say that part out loud. Scarlett's body had tensed.

"I love you, too," Scarlett admitted, and she sounded a little bit afraid of that knowledge. "I think I have for a long time." She shifted, and with her shift Kam was also forced to move, until they were lying next to each other, gazing into one another's eyes. "Were you… Were you trying to scare Kyle off? I know that the two of you had never gotten along-"

"No! Oh, no, no no, no. I would never do that to you. If that's who you wanted, I wasn't going to purposefully get in the way of that." Kam paused, and she swished her mouth to the side as she considered. "He was a jerk, and I didn't want to be nice to him, but if he was your kind of jerk then I wouldn't interfere with that."

"Thank you," Scarlett said, and she shuffled closer to Kam, tucking herself under Kam's chin like she had done when they'd slept in the same bed. "I'm glad to know you trust my decision making skills. On the other hand, I'd hope you'd tell me if I were dating a complete asshole."

"If we're um, doing this stuff together? I think you should know that probably falls into the category of dating a complete asshole," Kam joked, but Scarlett lifted her head, frowning down at Kam.

"You are not a complete asshole," Scarlett said, and she pecked a kiss to Kam's mouth. "You are sweet and lovely and supportive and kind. You're wonderful."

"Oh yeah?" Kam asked, waggling her eyebrows. "You want to move this party to a bed and I can show you just how wonderful I really can be?"

Scarlett's answering grin was all that Kam needed in this whole world, but her words were an added bonus. "Hell yes."

CHAPTER SEVEN

"I don't know how I never noticed," Kam remarked. She was standing in Scarlett's room, looking around her at the decor. Specifically, the curtains. They were made out of bandanas and they were very definitely the bi pride flag colors. There were matching throw pillows on Scarlett's bed. She was struck again with how homey Scarlett's room was. The swirling iron bed frame with roses on each corner post, the pink quilt and the pale orange walls. Wait… "Aren't we not supposed to paint? Isn't that one of the rules?"

"It's fabric. I tacked it up with thumbtacks. Mr. Tsui will never know," Scarlett said with a smile. She was in the middle of unpacking her darling machine, freshly back from the repairman. She settled the vintage machine back on her white painted desk and gave it a loving stroke along the top with her extremely talented fingers. Kam was certainly learning to appreciate all the things Scarlett was capable of with her hands. The repair guy must have cleaned up the machine, too, because Ruby never looked better. Scarlett beamed. "There you are, baby, safe and sound."

Kam grinned at her, watching as she unpacked the cord that went with the machine from her farmer's market tote and set about plugging it in. First to the side of the machine, then to the wall. Scarlett's squeal of delight when the light flicked on was priceless. "She's happy to be home."

"It only took a week. I bet she missed us," Scarlett said in a teasing voice. She turned back to Kam and reached out to snag her wrist, pulling her close. She nuzzled under Kam's chin and pressed a kiss to her neck.

"And here I thought you might be more interested in doing something crafty tonight," Kam said. She brought her hands up to cup Scarlett's behind, clothed under a dress made from the softest bed sheet. "It's been a whole week."

And what a week. Without Kyle, or her sewing, Kam had Scarlett all to herself. The honeymoon phase was definitely real. There had been more relaxed evenings in front of the laptop, snuggled in watching movies (or not, as the mood struck them). There had been attempting to cook dinner together, bringing each other endless drinks during the work day and kissing during coffee breaks. Kam had never been happier.

"I really should," Scarlett murmured against Kam's skin. "I mean, in an ideal world, I would be getting that order ready for Gallery QC, but I don't think there's any time now. They wanted so many dresses by Monday. I'd have to sew through the whole weekend."

"Hey," Kam murmured, bringing her hands from Scarlett's lucious bum to grip her waist. She pulled Scarlett back so she could look in her eyes. "That's okay with me, you know that, right? If you need to take some time to get this done, I understand."

Scarlett offered Kam a grateful smile. It shouldn't have to be said, but she seemed thankful to have Kam on her side. "I'd have so much to do, though, and entirely alone. He really set me back."

Kam's head tilted to the side as she considered the idea that had popped into hre head. "What if you showed me?"

"What?" Scarlett's eyes were wide with surprise.

"Well, you know, I'm really sure I can't do any sewing, ever, and designing dresses is never going to be my thing, but I bet I can pin stuff, or do basic things," Kam said with a casual shrug. Scarlett was looking at her like she had just proposed. Kam swallowed nervously. "If that's- You know, if I- If I can help you."

"You'd really do that?" Scarlett asked. Kam grinned. Sweet Scarlett and her ridiculously huge, ruffled collar and her cartoon dress, wearing a necklace that had a little wooden diner-girl on it surrounded by wooden cartons of fries and milkshakes.

"Where in the absolute hell did you find that necklace?" Kam asked, cracking a smile. "It's so much."

"Too much?" Scarlett asked, and her fingers came to rest on the little figure. Kam shook her head.

"No, she's perfect," Kam assured her. "It's just very unique."

Kam knew that she was going to need to go slow with Scarlett in some respects. She would need to be encouraging and enthusiastic about the ways that Scarlett expressed herself. Scarlett was a brilliant artist, and she was so beautiful, and she was continually putting up with people who just didn't believe in her. Kam wanted to help her *shine*. Scarlett's answering smile was so bright, so thankful, and it told her everything she needed to know.

"I got it at that big thrift place over in Blue Goat Township," Scarlett said. She hopped over to Kam and pressed a soft kiss to her cheek. "Have I mentioned how happy I am that we're doing this?"

"Only like, five times since this morning," Kam replied, and she wrapped an arm around Scarlett's waist. She leaned in to breathe her words against the shell of Scarlett's ear in a way she knew would make Scarlett squirm. "Please never stop."

"I won't." Scarlett, her ball of sunshine, her creative, crafty girl, allowed about a minute of cuddling before she pulled back. "Alright! We've got work to do! I think I can do a majority of the actual stitching, but it's really the pinning and cutting that slows me down. If I could get your help with that, I bet we could get the order filled. How do you feel about ironing?"

"I'm all yours, Captain," Kam said with a jaunty salute.

"Quite," Scarlett said.

In the end, it was a long and tedious weekend, but Kam was satisfied. Scarlett was a patient teacher and carefully explained the answer to any question that Kam might have had. She was certainly learning an appreciation for what Scarlett did. Not that she didn't have one before, only it was different when you witnessed the effort that someone put into actually crafting something with their own hands. She guided Kam through carefully pulling loose stitches to create gathered skirts and ruffles, pinning each tiny pleat in place so that all the gathers were even when Scarlett sewed. At one point, Kam had to leave Scarlett stitching so she could go and pick up spare threads and pins from the fabric store over in Blue Goat.

She brought home takeout Indian food, complete with a mango lassi, because she knew it was Scarlett's favorite, and made her take a break to eat something.

"You're good at taking care of me," Scarlett told her softly when they were curled up in bed later. At one in the morning on Saturday night, or Sunday morning more like, Kam had forced Scarlett to put a literal pin in it and come to bed. The alarm was set for six in the morning on Sunday so they could keep going, but Kam had jammed her hands with the sharp pins too many times for her to be able to continue.

"You take care of me, too," Kam replied. "Happy to return the favor."

"I mean, if you're keeping score," Scarlett said, giving Kam a playful nip against her collar bone. Kam giggled. In the dark room, in her bed with Scarlett soft and pliant beneath her, Kam teased along the flesh of Scarlett's inner thigh.

"You want?" Kam asked softly. Scarlett gasped as Kam's fingers trailed that sensitive spot where her thigh joined her hips. She was teasing a gentle stroke against other parts of Scarlett, too.

"Always," Scarlett breathed. Kam dove beneath the covers and set to work. With slow determination, Kam kissed and sucked her way down, until Scarlett was coming with Kam's fingers buried inside her and Kam's mouth on her clit. Blissed out, and entirely comfortable, Scarlett was snoring soon. Kam smiled. This could be fucking perfect, if they were careful with one another.

They made the deadline. Well, minus two dresses, which Gallery QC gave them an extension on. They celebrated with lattes from Devil's.

"Ew, is that Frankie?" Kam asked Quita as she waited for

their drinks. She'd parked Scarlett at a table inside, where the air conditioning was blasting because It was impossible to avoid on a day this fucking hot. She glanced from the register, where Quita was, down to the end where Eve was gently instructing a pink-haired girl in making drinks. Quita grimaced.

"It was *not* my idea to hire her," Quita muttered.

Frankie notoriously worked at the Cabin, one of the strangest gay clubs that Kam had ever set foot in. Not necessarily bad, but it's remote location in the middle of the woods in the mountains had always set Kam on edge. Like being in a horror movie. Like something was waiting to ambush her.

"Did she quit the bar?" Kam asked. Quita shook her head.

"Nah, just needed extra cash to make rent," Quita said. Her frown deepened. "Everything has been slow with the pandemic."

"Everything except Devil's," Kam said. She was attempting cheer, but she knew it was forced. Quita nodded.

"Everything except Devil's," she echoed. Kam waved to her as she moved to the end of the counter to pick up their drinks from Frankie. Strange girl. She shivered as she walked back to Scarlett.

"Frankie works here now?" Scarlett asked, taking her iced latte from Kam. She nodded.

"Yeah, it's weird, right?"

"I don't know. She always seemed nice to me," Scarlett said with a shrug. "I kissed her once."

"Seriously?" Kam's voice was high with surprise as she slid into the seat across from Scarlett.

"Oh yeah, during Pride, the year before the lock down. We were both really drunk, though," Scarlett said, as though she had to explain why she would have kissed anyone other than Kam. As if just a week ago she hadn't been sucking face with Kyle. Kam smiled at her.

"That's cool, I guess. Was she good at it?"

"Eh. I've had better. Especially recently," Scarlett said, waggling her eyebrows at Kam. She wasn't very good at it and ended up doing something with her whole forehead that made her space buns jiggle.

"Flatterer," Kam teased. "You wanna go home? I'm sure you're tired. I am."

"In a second. I'm gonna give Frankie one of my business cards," Scarlett said. "She commented on that last post that she might want a custom order."

"Awesome!" Kam watched her walk towards the counter, leaning on it to talk to Frankie. She sipped her drink. Was there a flare of jealousy? Maybe a little, but if Scarlett said it was nothing, it was nothing. She needed to trust Scarlett. Besides, they'd literally thrown her ex-boyfriend out together, which was a helluva bonding experience. Quaint City was a small town. They were sure to wander into one of Kam's exes eventually.

Scarlett was bounding back to the table, smiling brightly. "She wants a dress with mermaids on it. It's gonna be so fun. You ready? I have so many plans for you today."

Kam almost choked on her drink from laughing. "You sure? If you're tired..."

"Oh, you're right. I'm so tired. I'm going to need to spend all evening in bed, with you there, just to make sure I definitely don't get up," Scarlett said. Kam cackled.

"You got it, honey," Kam said. She stood and Scarlett reached out to take her hand. They were going to walk home together, hand in hand, and then Kam was going to do her damndest to keep Scarlett in bed.

All night long..

UPCYCLE MY HEART

CHAPTER ONE

It had been over a month since Erin had packed all her stuff and left.

The problem with moving in with someone who had already been living on their own for a long time was that, when they moved out, you realized just how many holes they were carving into your heart. It wasn't just the obvious, person-shaped hole that was missing, it was stuff, too. It was the fact that when Denver first tried to fry an egg the morning after, there hadn't even been a pan to cook with except the one small saucepan they liked to use when they made ramen. They'd made an emergency run for a few essentials, coffee maker, frying pan, some cheap as shit silverware, but replacing an entire apartment was something they couldn't really afford to do. The morning where they'd stripped the bed only to realize Erin had left them with one set of sheets was uncomfortable. Denver had spent that particular evening on a bare mattress, googling which laundromats were open because of the pandemic.

With the pain of the break-up, they really hadn't been paying attention to the other stuff as much. Week after week, coming home to an empty apartment had seemed fitting. The bare walls matched the emptiness that Denver felt.

For fuck's sake, why couldn't they just-

Denver didn't want to complete that sentence.

Through everything that had happened in the world, that giant C word that no one seemed to want to say out loud anymore, Denver had reevaluated everything that they knew about themselves. Their time on this Earth suddenly felt too short to continue as they had been. Like so many queer adults,

Denver started to understand that they just couldn't live a lie anymore.

Okay and maybe spending a little time on social media had given Denver this cloud of optimism. Watching only the happy coming out videos could really blind you to how badly a partner might react to a 'sudden change' (that really was not at all sudden). Denver had come out. Erin had shit a brick.

They sighed. The sofa was one of the few pieces of furniture that Erin had left. Denver really didn't care at the time - take it all, they didn't want to be reminded of the relationship that was supposed to end in marriage and a family. She'd left the couch out of convenience. None of her friends had a truck big enough to move the thing, and damn if Denver was volunteering any of their friends.

They turned over and started to survey the room. From where Denver lay, they could see the entire apartment, except for the bedroom and the bathroom. It was one of those one bedrooms that had an open kitchen, separated from the living room by a half-wall. It was barely any bigger than a studio, really, and they'd spent the entire pandemic crammed in here with Erin. There were hardwood floors, at least, which meant it was easy to sweep, so Denver didn't have to replace a vacuum cleaner, and there were two big windows against one wall so it got a lot of natural light. they couldn't see the tiny hallway that led to the small bedroom and bathroom from where they were, it was behind them, but they knew it was just as bland. The emptiness itched at Denver's chest, about where their heart was.

They heaved a sigh.

It wasn't that Erin didn't have some valid arguments. Denver was almost forty and typically dressed exactly as they did in high school. In fact, a lot of their clothes were the same. When one was a metal head, one could usually just throw a patch or a safety pin over a hole and keep wearing the same shirt until it literally disintegrated. Denver owned a few plain shirts and pants, from the Before Times when they would still go into the office, and that might have been the start of the problem with

Erin. Their first date had been directly after work, and that probably gave her a false impression of what Denver was really like. And at first, during their honeymoon stage, that hadn't been so bad. But Denver showing up for brunch with Erin's friends in their black tee shirts and ripped up jeans (they had, at least, retired their bondage pants after college), was too much for her. She started to pick. And pick. And pick.

"I don't understand why you can't just keep wearing pants. Just be the guy," Erin had snapped during one desperate moment. She had regretted it, Denver knew that she had, but it put all the little things into perspective.

"God dammit," Denver said, squeezing their eyes shut. They didn't want to be sitting around on a perfectly good Sunday afternoon thinking about Erin or the shitty way she'd reacted. They didn't want to be reliving all the times they could have, *should* have, changed to make her feel more comfortable. They'd chosen the path of authenticity and they needed to live with the consequences. Even if the consequence was being single and probably undateable.

They pushed themselves into a seated position and huffed a sigh.

The thing was, they didn't want to look like this anymore either. They just didn't know how to translate themselves into their new identity.

"This is fucking depressing," Denver complained to the empty space. Fuck, even the area rug was gone, so their complaints had an almost echo-like quality to them. "Erin has been gone for a month. It's time to move on."

They stood and went into the bedroom, which was another disaster.

Erin had claimed the bed, which was fine, but that left Denver with a sad little mattress on the floor. No nightstand of which to speak, which was okay when Erin was there because she liked a 'clean minimalist' style, but Denver actually thought side tables were pretty handy, for drinks of water in the night or leaving books on. So maybe they needed one.

It would suck to give up the apartment entirely. It wasn't right in downtown Quaint City, but it was close enough that Denver could walk to Devil's Stomping Grounds, a queer book-and-coffee shop, or the other little businesses in the market area. But there were so many echoes of Erin here, it seemed like they were going to have to.

After they settle this decor thing, they should really donate all of their clothes. Clean start. Entirely eco unethical, and Jesse would throw an entire shit fit, but fuck him. He wasn't the one dealing with a break-up.

Denver sighed and scratched at their jaw, unable to decide if their stubble was giving them dysphoria or not. Essentially, they were pretty sure they were just going out of their mind.

Adulting was a marketing scam and Denver was about to buy in. If life was just selling a commercial of commercialism, then bring on the credit card debt because Denver was ready to spend. It felt... dirty. But that also felt kind of good.

They opened their closet and started pulling things out. Tee shirts and jeans puddled on the mattress with soft swishes of fabric. They left their work clothes still hanging up because they were needed but then, when they turned to look at the mess on their bed, they decided to throw those in, too. After five minutes of passionate ripping, they stopped and surveyed the damage. And then they bent and picked up a tee shirt. It was soft, and the fabric had started to wear so that little pin-prick holes were dotting the shoulder and the hem. The black had long faded to a brown-gray color that made them feel a little sad, but also comforted because the texture was just so buttery and smooth. Maybe this one could stay.

With a sigh, they started painstakingly hanging all of the clothes back in their closet. One by one, boring button up shirt and worn-through-the-crotch jeans were placed back on the hangers and then put away, neat and tidy. Just because one was an aging millennial punk didn't mean they had to be messy as well.

With a soft sniffle, Denver looked around at the room which

had seen a disaster and then returned to it's normal shape, clean and sparse. It was how Denver felt, honestly. Denver had seen this big change, but no one noticed. There was nothing different about them, nothing that proved the damage that Erin had caused (or that Denver had felt when they'd decided to come out). And coming out hadn't made them feel any younger, either. They still had the same body, the same slight wrinkles around their eyes and the same silvering around their temples and scattered about in their facial hair. They scratched their chin again.

This whole thing fucking sucked.

Their skin itched with the desire to claw it off, and they knew they needed to get out of the apartment, but the pandemic still gave them so much anxiety that they were afraid. Denver's eyes fluttered shut, and they breathed in through their nose, out through their mouth. They needed a distraction. Something Erin would disapprove of would be perfect. Something they could focus on instead of all the other stuff going on in the world.

They opened their eyes, stomped out to the living room and grabbed their keys. With one more look at the empty apartment, Denver sighed and said one more time, "God dammit."

And then they left.

Quaint City was a small town in the middle of three connected towns - Quaint City, Wintervale, and Blue Goat Township. Quaint City was as picture perfect as it's name thanks to a recent marketing campaign to increase tourism. It was full of cobblestone streets with old-time street lamps, even though they ran on electricity they still looked vintage and cool. There was a creek that ran through all three towns, and the main street went beside it, which was annoying because that meant the road flooded when there was heavy rain. Wintervale had tried to capitalize on Q.C.'s adorability and kept all the big box stores out of it's city limits, except for a grocery store. This meant that if anyone needed something that couldn't be found in the artisan shops that lined Main Street, they had to drive all the way through Blue Goat Township. At the tail end of Blue Goat, there were a few big strip malls, and inside one of them was D.I.Y. Warehouse.

Erin had disapproved of D.I.Y. projects in general. Glitter would stick to things. Glue could be spilled and ruin their chance at getting a security deposit back. Paint was messy and Denver couldn't be trusted to pick something that wasn't black or some other hard-to-cover color.

Denver pulled their car into a spot far away from the other cars and leaned forward, letting their forehead rest against the fake leather. The air was blasting through the car, and it made them shiver. *In through the nose, out through the mouth. In through the nose, out through the mouth.*

They slipped their mask over their face and double checked that they had their wallet and their keys before leaving their car and starting towards the store. The sun was impossible. At least in downtown Quaint City, there were picture perfect little trees every so often, which provided some coverage from the oppressive summer sun. Maryland was known for it's humidity and more often than not the air felt thick enough to swim through. Thankfully, summer was almost over, but it would still be another month until the air wasn't actively trying to hurt people.

Why were there so many people out this late on a Sunday?

The store was crowded, full of shoppers both wearing a mask and not, which confused the ever-loving fuck out of Denver because there were literal signs everywhere asking people to be safe. It was like no one cared, which rubbed at Denver's heart in an uncomfortable way.

It was a lot. It was intimidating. Denver stood for a second, right in the middle of the entranceway, and tried to breathe but every time they did, the mask stuck to their mouth. It felt like being suffocated. They weren't an asshole, they knew why the mask was needed, but it was still uncomfortable to wear. Denver managed to take another step forward, and they flexed their hands nervously at their side. Why were they even here?

There was noise. Unmasked children were screaming, begging their parents for one thing or another. Parents were arguing with each other as well as their off-spring. No one paints a kitchen orange, Roland. No one puts an entertainment center in a bathroom, Jodie. Much like Jimmy in aisle seven, whose parents were trying to bribe loudly enough Denver could hear them halfway across the store, it was beginning to feel altogether too much. Denver's palms were beginning to sweat, and they had enough sweat pooling at the base of their spine that they felt it start to drip down their asscrack, which made them so much more self-aware. Their heart raced.

Denver let their eyes flutter closed and tried once more to inhale through their nose, letting the breath out through their mouth slowly. How slowly was slowly enough?

A soft, quiet voice spoke from nearby. "I find it helpful to imagine bees."

Denver's eyes opened and they looked down. A woman stood in front of them. She was almost as tall as they were and, sure enough, her mask was a pretty color blue with tiny little bees printed all over it. The eyes that peered over her mask were warm, inviting. Like the perfect temperature controlled hot-tub on display in aisle twelve. Her hair was swept into a ponytail that stuck out of the hole in her D.I.Y. Warehouse baseball cap.

"Bees?" Denver asked, trying not to wince at how condescending they sounded.

The woman nodded. "Bees. They're really cute, if you can concentrate hard enough on it. They're yellow and black, and really fuzzy, and they even have little toes. Sometimes they're covered in so much pollen that it falls off of them like a dusty cloud. And we'd die without them. So, yeah. Whenever I start to struggle, I close my eyes and imagine this little bee in a tulip and all you can see is his pollen-covered-butt sticking out."

Denver's lips twitched under their mask. "Do you talk to all of your customers about the anatomy of bees?"

The woman, whose name was Celia if the tag on her apron was correct, nodded and she smiled, as evident by the sweet lines that appeared by her eyes. "I like bees."

Denver's lips twitched again. "You don't find the buzzing annoying?"

"Well," Celia said thoughtfully, "when your thoughts are all buzzing anyway, it's not really like you notice." She straightened up. "Are you here for something specific? I could help you find it."

Denver paused for a second, letting their head fall to the side. "If I said I wanted insect poison? Maybe bee-specific?"

Celia snorted. "I get paid minimum wage to assist people in finding what they need. If that's what you're looking for, I'm contractually obligated to assist you."

Denver grinned. "But, you'd be judging me the entire time, wouldn't you?"

Celia nodded, "Oh, absolutely."

Denver liked her. From her name, to her pronouns (written in glittery marker under her name on her name tag), to the pin for Hatchet Grannies, a local band, on the side of her cap, she was delightful. Someone that would fit well with Denver's group of ragtag friends.

"I'm Denver."

"Nice to meet you, Denver. I'm Celia."

"I know," they said. "It's on your apron."

"Don't let the apron fool you. Last week, I left mine in my car and I was 'Tim' for a whole afternoon because that's who was forgetful enough to leave theirs in the break room," Celia said. "Are you feeling better?"

"It's all very-" Denver shrugged and then shoved their hands into their pockets. "Overwhelming, I guess. I just broke up with someone-"

"The worst."

"True," Denver agreed, but that didn't feel quite right. "We um, had an apartment together but now I'm alone in it. It's empty and feels it, so I thought I'd come and get some new furniture. But, um…"

"It's okay," Celia said gently. "It's overwhelming in here on a good day. You're doing great."

Denver smiled and nodded. "I thought I could handle it all, but I guess I can't."

"It's 'unprecedented times'," Celia said, and she made air quotations with her fingers as she spoke. "None of us are handling it. And hey, you're pretty brave! You came to a home improvement store on a weekend. That's a massive step outside of literally everyone's comfort zones."

"Well, Erin took most of our furniture. I'm getting desperate. A bed frame would be nice," Denver said with a small shrug. "I just want it to feel like me, you know?"

"You've come to the right place, then," Celia said. "We've got paint and lighting fixtures, some furniture, although I don't know if anything right out of the box would be your style."

Denver frowned. "My style?"

"Everything is so beige," Celia explained. She tilted her head to the side like a puppy. "You don't look like the kind of person who loves beige."

"You're not wrong," Denver replied, but they wondered what that was supposed to mean. What about their appearance had given them away as a hater of beige? What had immediately put them in a category that Erin would have disapproved of? Oh, for fuck's sake, they were going to need a therapist to help them navigate this shit. Maybe the one that Tate saw. She seemed to be good about the wiggly-gender stuff.

"It's not a bad thing," Celia said hurriedly, and Denver guessed their knit brows had tipped her off that they were a little worried about the accuracy of her guesses. "No, beige can suck cock in hell, it's just you might be better off at a thrift store."

"Ah, well. It's Sunday and we're still kind of out in the country. They're all closed," Denver said. They had started to wander away from the front entrance, which was helping their nerves because there were less people the further away they moved. But it was all so… industrial. And not in a cool way, like decor-industrial, but sanitized. Like all the box store. Bland. White. Metallic. Clinical.

"What about an art project? Something to keep you occupied until you can make it out to a thrift store?" Celia asked. Her eyebrows raised and her eyes looked hopeful.

"Um, yeah, that could be okay," Denver agreed.

"Did you... have anything in mind? A theme, maybe?" Celia prompted. Denver started to shake their head, but paused when an idea occurred to them.

"I recently came out as non-binary, which is kind of frowned on at my age but it feels important to me. I'd love to do something to honor that," Denver told her. When Celia didn't answer right away, they said in a rush, "That's probably stupid and corny, I just-"

"No, wait, that's a good idea. What about storage needs? A blog I follow just did this awesome pride flag night-stand and I think it would be really cool to do something similar but for you," Celia said. Denver snorted.

"You still follow blogs?"

"Do you want my help or not?"

"I thought you were contractually obligated," Denver teased. A flush was rising on the rounded slope of Celia's cheeks but she looked like she was smiling.

"As I am at work and unable to retaliate, I will allow it this time," she said with a sniff.

"I do have a side table in need of a new coat of paint," Denver said with a shrug. "It's not a bad idea."

Celia brightened, and Denver's heart started to thud unevenly. "Wonderful! Let me show you some paint samples."

As Denver followed Celia over to the paint aisle, they had a moment where they knew that they'd probably follow almost anywhere Celia led them.

CHAPTER TWO

It occurred to Denver that there were too many "thems" in one apartment to keep from sounding weird grammatically, but that's what happened when you were trans and so were most of your friends. They, as in Denver, envied Tate's ability to just sprawl, which was currently being demonstrated by their position on Denver's bland couch. From a socialized psychological standpoint, it should have been backwards. Tate, socialized in the ways that women were typically taught, should have tried to make themselves small. Denver had grown up assuming that 'man-spreading' was a birthright, but here was Tate just spread out like butter across the toast-plain couch that occupied Denver's living room and Denver just envied them. Denver, regardless of label, had always attempted to make themselves smaller. Lesser. Like, if they were quiet enough, Erin would ignore the throwback tee shirts and metal music and focus solely on the boring person she met on their first date.

Denver was sick of doing that, regardless of gender. Well, kind of. They knew they wouldn't ever be like Tate, but they wanted to be whatever Denver-ized version of happy they could be.

"I miss the river," Tate was moaning.

"There's a creek in Q.C.," Denver pointed out. Denver was on the floor, in the middle of their living room, with a tarp spread over the carpet. They had a paintbrush in one hand and there was a blank canvas in front of them. They'd spent most of the week working on the side table project, but that hadn't been enough to satiate their D.I.Y. hunger after last Sunday, so they decided to try some wall art, too. Something small, to keep them distracted from thinking too much. Especially since their thoughts of Erin were quickly being replaced by an intriguing, smart, funny, creative salesgirl at their local D.I.Y. store.

"That stupid creek is barely a thing," Tate continue to lament. "There's not even fish in it!"

"There are fish in it," Denver replied calmly.

"Little fish. Sunnies. Not giant, monstrous carp things like in the Delaware," Tate said. They had their leg draped over the back of the couch, and the other dangling off with their foot touching the floor.

"You also complain about the Delaware. Constantly," Denver added. They decided to dip their naked paint brush into a blob of purple paint. Random shapes could be art, right?

"But I also miss it," Tate whined. "I set a whole series of stories around the Delaware and Penn's Landing."

Back in their younger days, Tate had managed to escape Quaint City and move off to what they called 'a Real City' - the capital letters were important, as well as apparent in Tate's manner of speech. After about a decade in Philadelphia, Tate had been forced to move back home and they never really wanted to talk about why, especially since Tate spent every waking minute of every day making it very clear they did not care for small town life.

"You said it smells like dead bodies in the summer and it's basically still summer," Denver said as they continued filling in their purple circle.

"I miss the smell of dead bodies," Tate wailed.

"God, you're lucky you're cute," Denver muttered under their breath.

"You're gonna put up with me because I put up with you for the last month complaining about tits for brains Erin," Tate said with a dramatic sniffle.

"Don't call her that," Denver scolded. "It's inaccurate. It makes her sound like she had a ton of boobs but she had small tits and large brains."

"Sounded good anyway," Tate said. They looked over at

Denver. "What are you doing?"

"Painting," Denver said patiently. They swirled a black line through the circle.

"Yeah. Why?"

Tate's entire personality, their brand, was the same delinquent petulance that a stereotypical highschooler who smoked in the bathroom and mouthed off at the geometry teacher might have, only Denver was fairly certain Tate was a few years older than they were. They'd never thought it polite to ask. Like Denver, Tate had come out later in life as non-binary, although if you asked them outright they'd claim to only be "half out" because of something to do with their living situation. Denver knew just enough to figure that it was probably a homophobic parent and probably best not to question it because Tate was a bear when angered.

It had actually been Tate who guided Denver through coming out, since Denver had never considered themself to be trans until Tate gently explained that some nonbinary people considered that label to fall under the trans umbrella. After that, there had been so many long Zoom chats and nights out on the patio at Devil's Stomping Grounds discussing gender, sexuality and a bunch of questions.

Tate was a pain in the ass. But, with the tiniest bit of patience, they could also be kind of wonderful.

"Settled on a last name yet?" Denver asked, in an effort to avoid the conversation about painting. There were so many reasons to paint. Because it looked fun, because a cute girl in a D.I.Y. shop had recommended it, because it would annoy Erin. Because Denver had never been allowed to explore... softer pursuits. Because they wanted to? It all felt so fragile that they weren't quite ready to verbalize why they were doing it.

"Not yet," Tate said, blowing out a loud breath and a sigh all at once. "I thought about Blackburn, because Tate Blackburn sounds like a fantastic author name, but Quita said there's some anti-gay politician in Tennessee with that last name and it soured it for me. I just can't seem to commit to anything. And they still dead name me at work, so it's not like it matters right now."

Tate looked over, their hair flopping in their eyes as they watched Denver dab on some yellow dots. "Are you going to keep Denver?"

Denver shrugged. "For now. I mean, I don't dislike my name. And Denver is pretty unique, so it's got that working in its favor. We're in the same boat where work is still using my current legal name."

"And you don't know what you'd change it to, anyway," Tate pointed out. Denver settled back on their heels and studied their painting for a minute as they considered that.

"Denver feels good. Like comfortable blue jeans," Denver said before deciding to add another, smaller purple circle. "I think if you want to change it, you should change it to whatever you want. But this works for me."

"I like Denver," Tate said approvingly. There was a moment of silence before they steered the conversation back to Denver's renovations. "So what are you doing, exactly?"

"Home improvements," Denver said. They paused and looked around the apartment. It was still pretty bare, but now they had their non-binary pride side-table and a couple of new throw pillows, one of which was under Tate's head. They were making wall decorations. It was going to be a long process, but it was a start.

"Okay, but why?" Tate asked again. Denver scowled at them.

"Because there's nothing in here that feels..." Denver trailed off with a sigh of their own. They felt weird saying it out loud. "There's nothing here that feels like me."

"Yeah, I guess it is pretty sterile in here. Like a hotel room," Tate observed.

"Erin liked that kind of stuff," Denver said with a shrug. "And I didn't really want to argue about it, so I just let her do her thing. That whole 'Millennial Minimalism' thing in the tens really hit her hard."

"Ew," Tate said. Denver actually kind of wondered what

Tate's style was. Clothing wise, they were all over the place and Denver often suspected they were doing what Denver was doing and still figuring it all out. Coming out was like going through a second puberty that none of them wanted. Was Tate's bedroom in the place they shared with their parents still decorated as it had been when they were a kid? Was it curated? Were there books?

What was Celia's place like?

If she followed all of those blogs, would it be nice? Highly decorated? Did she do projects like Denver was currently doing? Tate was looking at Denver with skeptical eyes.

"Have you ever done... art before?" Tate asked with a grimace. They were judging Denver. Hard.

"No," Denver said, letting the word trail off into a longer sound than it needed to be. "But Celia was really good at explaining stuff. So I'm sure I can, y'know, figure it out."

Tate's eyes lit up and they slid into a more upright position on the sofa. They looked down at Denver like a very smug, very judgemental god. "And who is Celia?"

Denver couldn't stop their cheeks from heating. "Just, um. Just a girl- a woman. I mean, she works at D.I.Y. Warehouse and she seems..."

Really sweet. Really kind. And like she would be really pretty under that mask. Denver wondered what her lips looked like.

"She seemed to know a lot," Denver finished quickly. Tate's cloud of smug glee grew.

"A nice D.I.Y. girl told you how to make pride art," Tate said, and they did glance at Denver's freshly painted side-table. "She was nice."

"Shut up," Denver said, furiously returning to their painting. They barely missed knocking an open container of purple over, which would have ruined the entire canvas. "Why do you look like that? Stop it."

"Because a nice girl is giving home renovation advice to the disaster queer who said they'd never date again just last week," Tate crowed, with an added 'whoo-ooo-oo' in a high pitched voice that had Denver considering throwing a paint roller at them.

"She was cute," Denver mumbled.

"Of course she was. So, are you going to go back to D.I.Y. Warehouse?" Tate asked, waggling their eyebrows at Denver. "Maybe... pick up some paint samples? Need some sandpaper to rub your rough spot?"

"I hate you," Denver said, but they didn't mean it.

"I know," Tate replied with a grin. They were going to torment Denver with this knowledge for at least a week, if not a whole month. "But that still doesn't answer the question. What if she wants to show you her swatches?"

"Get out!" Denver said, but they were laughing, and so was Tate.

"Okay, fine, I'm going, I'm going. I have to meet Quita, anyway," Tate said. They stood and yanked their jeans up by the back belt loops to sit more comfortably around their hips. "I like you better angry than sulking. You coming tomorrow?"

"Coming where?" Denver asked. They decided their circle and line art might look better with some paint splatters, after all, so they picked up a brush and soaked it in white acrylic.

"Seven o'clock, Devil's," Tate said. They thrust their hands into the pockets of their worn jeans.

"Yeah, why not. I'll see you tomorrow," Denver said gruffly, flicking their paintbrush at their project. Tate snickered.

"I can't wait to tell Jesse you met someone. He's going to shit bricks," Tate said. "Does Celia know any way to repurpose bricks?"

"Oh God, get out!" Denver snapped. Tate just cackled, like the annoying friend that they were.

"Bye bye, lover D.I.Y.," Tate said as they sailed towards the door.

"That makes no sense grammatically," Denver complained. Tate only laughed harder.

"Neither do we," they said just before they let themselves out.

The next night, the patio outside of Devil's Stomping Grounds, the coffee shop slash bookstore that the local gays tended to gather at, was hotter than hell. The summer was clinging to Quaint City with claws, digging it's nails in and dragging it's scorching touch through the city. Denver once more had sweat pooling at the small of their back.

"Why are we outside?" Denver complained. Their hair was sticking to their forehead.

"Quita said the air is broken," Tate replied. "It's even hotter in there."

Denver looked over. The way that Devil's was situated was unique in that there was this weird little courtyard in the middle of Main Street and all the businesses faced into it. There was a platform-slash-brick-stage kind of thing, but there was also room for tables and chairs. Devil's took up the corner of one building, and then across the way was Vane Attraction and Gallery Q.C., which was an artsy boutique kind of place. The tables for Devil's were black and metal, which was not helping Denver in the heat. And Tate, like a complete freak, was drinking a hot latte. A ragged notebook sat in front of them.

"Writing something good?" Denver asked.

"Always," Tate replied enigmatically.

"Y'all." Jesse slid down into a chair next to Denver and then hissed as they registered how hot it was. "I just had the worst audition." He slumped over and buried his head in his arms.

"Yeah?" Tate asked, and their eyes met Denver as they both braced for what they knew was coming. Jesse had done a lot of community theater before the pandemic, and he'd struggled with it. As much as Quaint City thought it was a cultured, up and coming place, it was still rural in some aspects. Aspects which seemed to sting, if you were… different.

"Rejected. Probably before I even opened my mouth," Jesse complained. He sat up and scrubbed a hand down his face. "The director did one of these the second I walked in and I knew it was over."

He demonstrated a long head to toe look that ended in a frown and a raised eyebrow. He added in the swift glance to a fake audition sheet in his hand followed by more frowning. "I mean, I know I'm up against cis men, but this sucks."

"Suffering is a part of the artistic process?" Tate suggested.

"Yeah, but I'm starting to get more suffer and less art," Jesse complained. It was a valid complaint. They'd heard every excuse under the sun but it all came down to one underlying theme- You're not Welcome Here.

"What about that musical? You were really excited about that," Denver pointed out as they took a sip of their iced tea. Jesse's scowl deepened.

"Ah. Yeah. That one," Jesse said, and they huffed out a huge breath. "The director was good, and she said she was open to any casting, but the playwright's estate had it in the contract that the only way a trans person could get a role was if they auditioned for their assigned gender at birth. I'm tired of playing matriarchs."

"That fucking sucks, dude. I'm sorry," Tate said, and they actually looked sincere, which was a rarity for them.

"I mean, I expected it, when I really considered transitioning, but I didn't think it was going to suck this much," Jesse complained.

"You'll get there eventually," Denver tried to add hopefully, but they knew how hard it was for Jesse. The conservative streak that ran through Quaint City was strong. There were tiny bastions of hope, like the queer little courtyard where they all were sitting, but it was a small haven from a larger problem.

"I mean, it's not like I want to be famous or anything," Jesse said with a shrug. "I just want to act in plays and make cool art with my friends."

"Not me," Tate said with a cheeky grin. "I want to be famous."

Denver snickered, delighted that Tate walked into that one. "Untrue. If you wanted to be famous, you wouldn't be writing fanfiction. You'd be out there publishing original stories."

"Fanfiction is original," Tate said, and their lips pulled into a sulky bow. "Every story is technically fanfiction. Half the fun is trying to figure out what fandom the author wrote for before they changed the names and pretended they created something new. Besides, maybe my definition of fame is being a B.N.F., not monetary success."

Denver and Jesse blinked at each other before Jesse was brave enough to ask. "What the fuck is a B.N.F.?"

"Big name fan," Tate said smugly.

"It stands for 'write an original story and get paid instead of just giving stuff away'," Denver muttered.

"I can't believe I'm getting shit out of you," Tate said with a raised eyebrow. "After Erin gave you all that crap about growing up and not wearing your docs anymore, saying shit like 'you're too old for punk rock', *you're* going to make fun of *my* hobbies? You're in a glass house with a fistful of rocks, my friend."

"Hey!"

The Unofficial Trans Alliance of Quaint City all collectively turned towards the loud greeting being shouted at them from the front of Devil's Stomping Grounds. Denver blushed as they realized that Celia was standing there, waving, with an iced coffee in hand. It had taken them a moment- since everyone was outside, no one was wearing a mask, and they weren't used to a cute girl addressing them in public. Denver was unable to stop their face from splitting into a grin.

A grin that Tate was eating up with a spoon.

"Shut up," Denver warned.

"Is that Celia?" Tate sang, drawing Celia's name into at least four syllables.

"Shh, I'm going to kill you, she's coming over," Denver hissed.

"Hey!" Celia said cheerfully as she bounded up to their table. "How are you? How are your projects going?"

"Uhhh, y'know. Good," Denver said with a hard swallow. Tate snickered.

"A real Picasso," Tate murmured. Jesse poked them.

"Pick someone else, he sucks," Jesse said. Tate frowned.

"As a person or as an artist?" Tate asked.

"Both. Do some research," Jesse replied. Celia fidgeted as she watched their exchange. He extended a hand to her and said, "Hey, I'm Jesse. He/him pronouns, please."

"I'm Celia," she said. "She/her. I'm new in town."

"Very new," Tate said with an appraising grin that was made to make Denver jealous. "I'm Tate. They/them, if you please. Welcome to Hell."

"What?"

"Ignore them," Denver said, and they shot Tate a glare that hopefully communicated a 'be nice' message. "Tate is allergic to cuteness. Adorable small towns give them hives."

"It must be difficult for them to be friends with you, then," Celia said softly, taking a coy sip from her drink. Denver blushed.

"Nah," Tate drawled. "I get shots."

Thankfully, Celia laughed, so Denver decided that Tate could live to see another day. "I'm sure you do."

"And here I thought those were to prevent rabies," Jesse snickered.

"It's an all in one shot," Tate replied darkly.

"So," Denver said quickly, turning to Celia, "Night off?"

"Yeah. I was about to wander in the direction of the creek. Seems like a nice night for a walk." It seemed like a hideous night for a walk. The air was as oppressive as the mostly white and straight town council. "I saw you and thought I'd say hi. Check in with how your projects are coming. I really enjoyed talking to you the other day."

"Would you... like some company?" Denver asked, looking up at Celia. She smiled, and Denver knew she'd been hoping that they would ask that very question.

"I'd love some," she said, and she took another sip where the white-and-red striped paper straw lingered against the full curve of her lower lip. Denver blushed again.

"Don't go! I promise I've been trained not to bite," Tate said. They winked at Denver.

Denver pushed up to their feet and leveled a finger at Tate

and Jesse, wagging it gently. "You two kids behave. We're going on a walk."

"Ughhh, never," Tate scoffed. They looked entirely too smug to be truly hurt. Denver knew they were never going to hear the end of this.

Celia and Denver walked side by side for a little while in a comfortable yet also nervous sort of silence. The air was hot because it was summer, but it was heavy with something else. Possibility, maybe? Tate was the writer, not Denver.

"Your friends seem nice," Celia said quietly, wiggling her cup so the ice made crinkly noises against the sides. Denver smiled and gave a nervous shrug.

"My friends seem deranged," Denver told her. "Don't worry, they'll go back to the asylum eventually."

"They seem nice," Celia repeated, as if by saying it twice she would be cementing the 'niceness' as fact. "It must be a good place to be."

"There are some good parts to living here. There are some bad parts, but there are definitely some okay parts," Denver said. They offered her a shy smile. Her answering grin was smug.

"I look forward to finding more of the good parts," she murmured and she took another lingering sip from her straw.

"Whuhh-um, What brought you to Quaint City?" Denver asked. They arched their brows. "Was it work?"

"Oh, no, boring old story." The main market street of Quaint City had a creek that ran through it. It actually connected all three of the towns, but Quaint City was the only one that had a picturesque path running along the water, winding through a few charming side-streets with more small businesses. It would have been almost romantic except for the part that in the summer, the creek smelled like a dead body. Celia seemed to be pretending it didn't. "I broke up with someone and I just felt like a change of scenery might be a good idea. My mom used to live here when she was younger, so I thought it might be a good quiet place to spend some time."

"And how's that scenery working out for you so far?" Denver

asked. Celia wrinkled her nose at them.

"Well, the images are fine. The smell, though," Celia giggled. "You could have warned me."

"I think that the creek of eternal stench is something everyone has to experience for themselves. Just think, you're closer to becoming one of us," Denver said with a shrug. Celia giggled harder.

"Creek of eternal stench, oh my God. So, a Labyrinth fan, then?" she asked. Denver nodded.

"More like a Bowie fan," they confirmed. "God, what an aesthetic, am I right?" She was nodding back.

"Absolutely," she agreed. They fell into a slightly awkward silence as they continued. Several moments passed before she spoke again. "It was a few months ago. My break-up, I mean. I've already talked my friends' ears off about it. He wanted kids, I didn't. It was pretty amicable, but still hurt."

"Ah, yeah, I, uhh, I can relate to that," Denver admitted. They pitched their empty cup in a trash bin as they passed and then shoved their sweaty hands into their pockets. "My ex was pretty upset when I came out as non-binary. She really wanted that picket-white-fence kind of life, even though that's just like, this marketing scam our society has been sold. Even if it was true, I don't think that kind of life would make me happy. I mean, maybe I'm selfish but I think it's okay to want to just focus on making yourself feel good rather than trying to fit into some box just because we're 'supposed to'."

"Technically, by breaking up with her, you made both of you feel good in the long run. She'll find that picket fence and you'll get to be everything you want to be," Celia said softly. "Some people will just drag that kind of stuff out and really make you miserable in the end. You didn't pretend you were something you weren't only to wake up ten years later and realize it wasn't what you wanted."

Denver looked over at her with a teasing smile. "And how long were you and your ex together?"

Celia winked. "A decade or so. Give or take."

"Day-um, that is a long time," Denver said with a low whistle.

"So... any painting questions? You've got a resident home improvement expert on your side," Celia said, after they'd passed another few moments in silence. Denver wanted to believe it wasn't awkward, but they were two people who were just getting to know one another. They were bound to have some lapses that were a little strained as they learned about each other.

"It's hard because I'm still figuring it out. I'm not really sure about my personal style, much less my decor style. And Erin took so much with her when she left, it's a bit sparse," Denver said. They shrugged. "I didn't bring much with me in the relationship, I guess."

But it had been hard. Denver hadn't had anything, and Erin had already possessed so much as far as furnishings, so the entire apartment had basically been in her control. She hadn't seen the point in going out and doing things together to make their nest more of a combination. Why would she? It was a waste of money when she already had perfectly good things they could use. Denver hadn't really fought it out.

"Tell me what kind of things you like," Celia prompted gently.

"Well, one of our biggest fights was because I like things I still liked when I was in highschool. I like metal music and skulls and punk rock," Denver said. They looked down at the rancid creek for a second, watching the large dark shapes of the fish swimming below the surface. "But, you know, Gerard Way grew up, changed aesthetics. I don't know what my grown-up punk is like."

"But she told you it didn't involve skulls?"

"Oh yeah," Denver agreed, and they looked back at Celia. "I don't even know what to wear most days, how am I supposed to figure out my decor style? I feel... confused."

"I think that's a valid way to feel. You're doing something really brave at a very up in the air time in your life. That's hard," Celia told them. Her lips swished to the side. "You know what you need?"

"What?" Denver asked.

"A thrift store," Celia told them. "What are you doing tomorrow morning?"

"I'm open," Denver said before wondering if they should have hesitated. Did they seem too eager? A Saturday morning in a thrift store with Celia did sound exactly like what they needed.

"Let's meet at Devil's Stomping Grounds at, say, eight? If that's not too early? We can grab some coffee and I can take you to this place I found, it's got some really cool stuff." Celia grinned hopefully at them. "That sound okay?"

Eight a.m. sounded like death, but Denver found themselves nodding. "That sounds amazing."

"Cool," Celia said with a happy little wiggle. They had crossed from the creek down one of the more residential streets. It was a little run-down. Several of the buildings had peeling paint and were real fixer-uppers. Celia pointed to a peeling blue painted brick number they were approaching and said, "This is me. So, I'll see you tomorrow?"

"Yeah, of course," Denver said, and they looked up at her building. "You live here?"

"Yeah," Celia said, and she grinned the slyest smile. "You oughta know by now I love a good fixer-upper." She reached out to squeeze their hand and then went inside.

Denver smiled and started the long walk back to Devil's Stomping Grounds. They had a date. With Celia.

CHAPTER THREE

Getting dressed in the morning was turning out to be more mental health points than Denver actually had in their arsenal. There were the usual hurdles, of course. Things like, "Am I allowed to even care what I look like? Do I risk doing something other people will perceive as different?" There were also the things like, "I'm going out with a very cute girl who I would like to look attractive for, but what if her idea of attractive is different from mine?" It was all a bit of a mess, really, and they ended up settling on a pair of plain blue jeans that were just a bit too big on them and a loose tee shirt for their favorite metal band. It wasn't quite the look they were going for, but honestly, if they were clawing their way through the donated furniture of a thrift store, it was probably good enough. Denver knew that was probably part of the problem. What was even 'good enough'?

So, suffice to say, when they arrived at Devil's, they were not in the best of moods. And mostly because they'd talked themselves in too many circles before they even left the house.

But it helped that Celia's smile was bright and eager. Her eyes were sparkling and she was happy to see them. Denver couldn't help but grin back. Celia had chosen a plain ribbed tank top in a really blushy dark pink, and a pair of paint-splattered jeans, with sandals. Even though it was early in the morning, it was already hotter than Satan's asshole, so her skin glistened just a bit with a light sweat. Denver hoped that she hadn't been waiting for them too long.

"Good morning, sunshine!" Celia said happily as Denver came closer. They gave into the urge to open their arms and she happily leapt into them for a hug.

"Is that what this time of day is called? I'm not familiar with it," Denver said as they released her. She wrinkled her nose.

"I should have known you were a night owl," she said. "I would be, too, but they've had me on the morning shift a lot lately. I think I'm getting used to it."

Denver shrugged. "It's okay if you are just a morning person, too. I won't think any less of you."

Celia smiled, but she didn't reply to that. She motioned to the shop. "Shall we? Maybe once we have caffeine, you'll be more appreciative of the time of day." She pulled her mask out of her shorts pocket and slipped it over her face. It was a bright, rainbow type of plaid. Denver beamed before covering their own face in the leftover surgical mask they'd swiped from a big box store.

"Doubtful," Denver teased. They, the plural they, went into the shop and Denver let out a groan. A Saturday morning at Devil's Stomping Grounds was crowded, even during pandemic times, and it didn't help that Frankie was on the espresso machine with Quita nowhere to be found. The line was backed up to the door. "This line is impossible."

"Would you rather go somewhere else?" Celia asked, biting her lip. Denver shook their head.

"No, it's just the girl that usually works this shift isn't in and that girl is new. It's going to be a while, but I don't mind the wait," they told her. Celia smiled.

"I don't mind waiting, either. It's nice to wait for good things," Celia replied. "And I can tell you, this is the best coffee I've managed to find."

Denver nodded. "Eve is the owner, and she's really good about where they source the beans from. Quita has worked here longer than anyone. She should really be a manager now, since she usually runs the place when Eve isn't here. Frankie is okay. She tends bar over at the Cabin-"

"What's the Cabin?" Celia asked. Denver snickered.

"The weirdest gay club you'll ever be in. It's all the way out in the country, halfway up a mountain, and it's decorated like something out of frickin' Twin Peaks." They pretended to frown. "You're not planning on decorating my place like a ski lodge, are you?"

Celia laughed. "No, I'm not. Although, now that you mention it, black and white chevron-"

"Chevron had its time in the mid-two-thousands," Denver replied, and Celia giggled again. Only, this time, she put her hand on Denver's arm and squeezed. It caused Denver to blush, and then gulp. "We're trying to update it, not send it back a few decades."

"I'm glad you have some idea of what we're doing, because I'm just here for the ride," Celia teased. They had inched closer and closer to the start of the line, where Max was waiting to take their order.

"No food truck today?" Denver asked with surprise. Usually, Max ran a food truck down at the Quaint City farmer's market on the weekends. Which explained, just a tiny bit, why they- oh, gosh, another they- were running the register when Frankie was making the drinks. Drinks could be remade, but screwing up the drawer could take forever to fix for a new person. Max used to work part-time at the coffee shop before saving up enough for their truck, so they knew a little bit of how to run things.

"Nah, Eve called in a favor. Quita isn't feeling well, and she's testing negative but Eve still wants her to quarantine," Max said.

"What about Eve?"

"Oh, she's out of town. And since it's the one time in the entire year she gets a single weekend off, I'm frankly proud of her for reaching out and protecting that time for herself. It's hard being a business owner," Max said, as if anyone was surprised by this. Although, they might have been. They might not have realized the time commitment to running a food truck.

"I'm guessing by your appreciation of her boundaries that you've started seeing Honey, too," Denver said, their lips twitching under their mask.

"Ah, yeah, Tate recommended her," Max replied. They slumped guiltily, and gave a sigh. "I tried to get Cordie to see her with me but she said no. She needs time, apparently, and I didn't reply to that because how do you reply to that? If I text, I'm not giving her time. If I don't text, how does she know that I'll still be here when she's ready? If I do text, I'm a doormat, if I don't, I'm... a jerk, maybe."

"Hey! Move it along!"

The man standing behind Denver made them jump with the agitation in his voice. Max was about to say something when Frankie called out, "Patience is a virtue, sir!"

"Oh, shit," Max muttered. "Um, okay, is that everything? Before a war breaks out?"

Denver and Celia ordered, and left Max to placate the guy that was super pissed about Frankie's lack of urgency in preparing anyone's drinks and Max's natural chattiness. Celia leaned in and asked, "Whose Cordie? Ex?"

"Ah, um, no it's weird," Denver confided as they waited for Frankie's slow but skilled hands to craft their lattes. "They were best friends in high school and they worked really hard together to save up and start a food truck, but then they had a falling out. To be honest, Max can be a bit short, especially under pressure and Cordie had some personal stuff happen. I think. I'm not as close with Cordie as I am with Max. It's like, they have a good customer service face but not a good method for dealing with close relationships."

"A meme friend," Celia said softly with a wise nod. Denver's brows knit together.

"What?"

"A meme friend. Someone who is really good at sharing cut-to-the-core, I-definitely-know-you-too-well memes, but who also is very awkward and probably on some kind of spectrum," Celia said. Denver chuckled. They couldn't disagree. How many nights had Max sent them some really relevant "It's okay to be nonbinary" meme on social media, somehow knowing after midnight that Denver would be up and in the middle of a gender crisis.

"That is very accurate," Denver said, and they took their latte from Frankie. It was suspiciously pink, but Denver wasn't about to complain.

"Is that- but you didn't get the strawberry, wait, didn't we just get normal iced coffees?" Celia asked.

"Do you want to be the one to tell her?" Denver asked with a nod at the hyper-chipper Frankie. "Hey, Frankie-"

"Hmm?" Her faded pink hair, which was taking on an orangish tone, was falling out of it's high ponytail. It framed her manic blue eyes, which popped against the pink cotton of her mask.

"Nothing! This is just so good, you're doing such a good job," Celia said quickly, and Denver had to cough to hide a laugh. "Did I get the same one? I can't remember what I ordered."

"Yup! The strawberry shortcake special," Frankie said confidently with just a hint of 'oh shit did I eff this up'. Denver coughed again and Celia elbowed them. "Was that wrong?"

"Nope! Just wanted to make sure," Celia said smoothly as she took her drink from Frankie. "Thank you! Hope it slows down for you!"

"Oh, no, never. I love it when it's busy," Frankie said cheerfully. "It makes the time go by faster."

"Definitely," Celia agreed. "You're so right."

They both waved to Frankie and then went for the door, barely able to contain their giggles. Once they were outside, Denver peeled off their mask with a gasping wheeze. "My God, you're such a liar! I'll have to be careful with you."

"I couldn't tell her!" Celia objected, swatting at their arm. "I'm not going to hurt her feelings if she's new, especially with that guy who was behind us. He's probably going to yell at her enough as it is."

Denver took a sip of their drink and regretted it, immediately. "Why does it taste like perfume?"

"That's um, that's not strawberry. I think she put rose syrup in it," Celia said, sampling her drink as well. The humid air was already starting to beat down on them, letting them know that while summer was on its way out, it was certainly going to put up a fight. "I can't do without coffee today. It's too early."

"Drive through?" Denver asked, waggling their eyebrows at her. She grinned and they both tossed their cups into the nearby trash can as they walked towards Celia's beat up truck.

"Absolutely," she said with a confident nod. Denver climbed into the passenger seat, closing the door with a rusty slam. As they pulled away, the angry man was coming out of Devil's with a pink drink in his hand.

"The problem with drive-through coffee," Denver said later, as they sipped at something from a chain restaurant, "is that it always has this weird, mustardy aftertaste."

"Things I'm learning about you, my new favorite friend, a list. First thing, you are a coffee snob," Celia teased. She parked her truck, something old and once painted blue before the rust had started to claim it, in the parking lot of one of Blue Goat Township's shady shopping centers. It was actually not too far from the one where they'd met. The pavement was cracked and had a few potholes that could be advertised as lakes in the B.G.T. Tourism brochure, if it had such a thing, and there were the usual suspects of stores- a dollar store, an off-brand grocery store, an Indian food place that Denver knew had the absolute best food, and an antique shop where the doctor's office used to be. In the biggest retail space was the thrift store, which already had a line out in front of it of early morning resellers looking for their next thrift score.

"I'm not so much a snob as I am just kind to my taste buds," Denver replied. They whistled. "That line is impossible."

"That's the second time you've said that this morning. Seems to be a theme." Celia seemed to hesitate by the front of her car. She twisted her hands in the hem of her tee shirt. "We don't have to, if you don't think you're up for it."

Was Denver up for it? They took a deep breath and looked up at the sky as they considered their options. Cute date, with a cute girl, even though it would be a tiny bit too much. They were pretty sure that Celia was looking forward to this, and they didn't want to disappoint her. Alternatively, they also didn't want to end up having a panic attack in the store because some inner demon convinced them that the man in aisle six knew they were queer just by how tight their skinny jeans were and that he was waiting to beat them up in the parking lot. Or, that the women with allergies at the register was actually contagious and Denver would catch the illness they were all trying to avoid. They looked over at Celia's cute little face.

Fuck it.

They pulled their mask out of their pocket, slipped the loops over their ears, and held out their hand. "I'm ready if you are."

They could be brave, for Celia. She grinned back at them and put her own mask on. Her hand slid into Denver's as though it had been meant to be there all along. Their fingers slotted perfectly together. "I'm ready."

The inside of the store was overwhelming, to say the least. Giant thrift stores like this had been popping up all over the state and putting the dingy, mom and pop style ones out of business. It was a little bittersweet for Denver. They hadn't done thrift shopping in a while, but they had some really nice memories of being a teen on a budget looking for hardcore clothes in dark corners filled with vintage leather and Levi's before hipsters realized that was a cool thing to do. On the other hand, having more options was nice. This place even had some flat carts that stores like D.I.Y. Warehouse used so furniture could be stacked safely on top and shoppers could keep looking.

"You know, I think I did this all wrong," Celia said thoughtfully as they perused the furniture offerings. "I didn't measure your apartment, or even look at the space. I'm a terrible decorator. I was just so excited to come out and spend time with you that I forgot all the usual steps to redecorating a place."

"Measuring... would have probably been helpful," Denver admitted. They tossed their hair out of their eyes as they considered what their apartment needed. "So, like, the basics I could use might be a bed frame, if we can find one. A coffee table. Possibly some art because my walls are super boring right now. They were boring before Erin took her stuff, but without anything they're just... I mean, I guess it's actually an improvement. Erin's style was very doctor's office waiting room. Generic. Once Covid hit, it even took on that medicinal smell with the two of us cleaning so much and trying to keep everything sanitized during lockdown."

Celia was trying not to giggle, but the shake of her shoulders gave it away. "Okay, but what's your style? What do you like?"

Denver blushed. Could they say death and skulls and 'stuff that looks like it's from a cemetery but make it chic'?

"Come on," Celia said, elbowing them gently. "You can trust me. I won't laugh."

"You just did!" Denver told her. She giggled.

"Yeah, but your ex's style sounds heinous. That has to be an excused laugh."

"It's just, you know, I don't know what I'm doing. And Erin, she's not wrong. Whatever it is I'm doing, I'm three hundred percent too old for it," Denver complained. They stopped by a desk and looked longingly at it. It was old, but definitely not an antique. A reproduction, probably. If it had been painted black, it would've looked like it was just out of a Vincent Price movie. Denver stroked their fingers along the wood. "I like rock and roll, skulls, punk but somehow polished. Maybe that makes me a goth. Dark Maximalist? Is that a style?"

"It can be, if you want. You can do anything, Denver," Celia said. Denver gazed down at the scars in the finish of the desk, avoiding her gaze.

"Can I?"

"Of course. Don't let someone who isn't even in your life anymore suck all of the joy out of it," Celia said softly. Her hand gripped their arm. "So... What about skirts and dresses?"

The conversation turning abruptly from furniture to clothes had Denver sucking in a surprised breath. "What?"

"Is the baggy metal tee and skinny jeans really your thing, or is that because you don't know what else to do?" Celia asked. She held her hands up, an apology bright in her eyes. "I'm not saying you need a makeover, not at all, but I did have a friend in my old town who transitioned when she was older and she needed some help with make-up just because she never knew what to do. If you're masc and non-binary, that's completely valid, I just-"

"It's fine," Denver said quickly, desperate to stop the conversation before Celia's apology got any louder than it already was. They cleared their throat. "You're not wrong. Skirts are cool, I'm into them. But I feel like they're all so flowy and femme, and that's not the vibe. Like, there's nothing wrong with that, but it doesn't feel very 'me'."

"Fair," Celia said. She squinted, clearly wanting to ask something but hesitating before doing so. "Do you want some help with that?"

Denver considered for a moment, and then they nodded. "Yeah. Let's keep looking for stuff for the house, but yes. I'd love help with that."

Once their flat little cart had been filled with too many things for Denver to really process, they found themselves attacked by an armful of clothes and shoved into the recently reopened, thank you, Covid, dressing rooms.

"I went for less Stevie Nicks and more avant garde," Celia called from the other side of the door as Denver got dressed. They turned to look at the outfit in the mirror and they were stunned, blown away, by how amazing they felt. They opened the door to show Celia. The shock must have still been present on Denver's face, because her smiling eyes took a frozen, self-doubting tilt. Denver wanted to reassure her, to do something, because Celia had managed to nail their style in just a few minutes when no one else who knew them had been able to help at all.

Don't get Denver started on one ill-conceived shopping trip with Tate. It was a disaster, to say the least.

The outfit screamed vamp. Denver had on a straight, midi-length skirt with their black Docs poking out of the bottom.

Celia had picked an oversized grey tee with the armholes cut to make it into a muscle tank. They had on a thick silver chain and a loose, oversized 80's black blazer. Their layered wolf cut was long and wavy, with the shaved bits by their ears giving a hint of Boy George but make it modern. They looked tough, and femme, and edgy. They felt like the kind of person who lived in a cool, dark apartment filled with antiques and creepy old dolls and plants. They felt like David Bowie and Noel Fielding and every corporate goth they'd ever seen all rolled into one.

They felt classy.

"Celia," they breathed. "It's perfect."

Even with the mask, the relief shone through on Celia's face as her eyes relaxed into a genuine smile. She stood on her tip-toes and plopped a black wide-brimmed hat onto their head.

"No. Now it's perfect," she said softly.

CHAPTER FOUR

As they drove into Quaint City, their stomachs started to rumble. After all, they hadn't had anything to eat at Devil's before they left and thrifting had taken most of the morning and some of the afternoon. Luckily, Denver knew of a great diner that served all day breakfast and Celia seemed intrigued. It was one of those tiny places that had been in Quaint City since the nineteen fifties, with silver siding and all of the booths up against the wall of windows. There was a counter with chrome stools that swirled and a jukebox that played old music. Denver was pretty sure it was still owned by the original family, too, but they couldn't be sure. The sign at the front said to seat themselves, and they did. At their table, they were able to remove their masks. Denver's heart sped up at the sight of Celia's smile, unguarded and unmasked.

"Now, you want to talk about being a coffee snob," Denver said, as the server placed down their drinks and walked away. "You cannot tell Quita this, mind you, but there is nothing in the world as wonderful as diner coffee."

"Ooo, she's gonna be mad. There may come a day when I use this information against you, you understand," Celia teased. Denver laughed.

"It's true! I don't know why, but diner coffee is better than any coffee I've ever had." Denver picked up their cup, having sweetened it just a bit, and took a grateful sip. Celia was studying them with a thoughtful gaze.

"You were a theater kid," she said. Denver almost choked.

"What?"

"The only people who say diner coffee is the best coffee

were theater kids. You're nostalgic for those three a.m. Denny's gatherings," Celia said with a knowing nod. She picked up her coffee, too, and took a sip. "I'd know. I was a techie."

Denver giggled. "Of course you were."

"I was! I did set designs and lighting and stage managed!" Celia said. She scowled at Denver. "You were Hamlet, weren't you?"

"No!"

"Senior year, Hamlet, and all the girls told you that they had sexy dreams about you," Celia said with a smirk. Denver shook their head.

"I was the Nanny."

"What?" Celia's eyebrows knit together as she tried to remember a nanny character in Hamlet. It was Denver's turn to smirk.

"We did Romeo and Juliet our senior year," Denver told her. Shock dawned on her face, and then delight and she started cackling.

"No!"

"Absolutely. Let me tell you, I don't think anyone was lusting after me in that outfit," Denver said with a chuckle. Celia seemed delighted, laughing with glee. Her cheeks were turning a sweet pink.

"You were a milf!" She giggled. Denver was so engrossed in her face, in her laughter, drinking in this new friend full of things to discover, that they missed the chime of the bells over the diner door. "You were an absolute milf, I bet."

"Probably not," Denver said. They caught movement as the person stepped through the door, looking over involuntarily, only to groan. "Good Lord."

Tate had just walked in. Instead of their usual jeans and a tee shirt, they were dressed in nice black slacks and a pressed blue button-down. They might have even been wearing make-up. At the very least, their eyes were accented in a way that seemed to involve eyeliner and mascara, the rest was covered up by a mask. Denver could tell by the way their eyes crinkled that they were smirking when they finally looked back.

"Having a craft club meeting?" Tate asked as they approached the table, giving a little skip. Their hands were in their pockets and they had a leather folder under their arm. Denver recognized it because Denver had one, too, for holding their resume when they went on job interviews.

"Shut up. What are you doing here?" Denver asked. They raised their eyebrows expectantly.

"Getting waffles," Tate snickered. Denver frowned.

"Dressed like that?"

"Why not? It's a good morning for waffles," Tate said, and they raised their eyebrows back at Denver. Where Denver's expression had been meant to communicate a 'please don't fuck this up for me' and just a hint of 'leave', Tate's was definitely more of a 'well, now, isn't this cozy'. "Actually, I'm interviewing here. They've got a waiter position open."

Denver's brows folded into a confused furrow. "Weren't you working in that medical office? The one Cordie works at?"

Cordie had been the one-time food truck partner to Max, and she was really sweet but she also had a day job as a receptionist at a primary care office. The job sounded like hell on earth. Max had tried it but ended up only lasting a few days before quitting to go work at Devil's. Denver watched Tate, seeing how Tate's eyes flitted guiltily away before coming back, their voice sounding sheepish when they answered.

"Yeah. I quit," Tate said, and they looked like the words tasted like bile.

"You weren't there that long. What about needing to save-" Denver pointed out. Celia's hand tapped on Denver's, causing them to look over at her. Her expression was sympathetic.

"I'm sure they tried," Celia said softly. She looked back up at Tate. "It's gotta be hard being in a medical office during this whole thing."

"Yeah, it wasn't easy," Tate said. They shrugged. "Anyway, it's not like I'm ever going to actually get out of this place. Might as well accept my fate and try for a job that doesn't make me want to… yeah, best not to finish that. I'm off!"

They waved good-bye and went back to the counter to let the host know they were there for an interview. After a moment, they were escorted into the back of the building and out of sight.

"Are they okay?" Celia asked gently. Denver shrugged.

"As okay as I've ever seen them. I think they have depression, but they're seeing a therapist." Denver huffed and then shrugged again. "I know they have a hard time with their family, who are all locals. Quaint City seems like a nice little gay friendly tourist trap, but we're still kind of out in the sticks and there's a lot of people here who don't really take kindly to 'alternative lifestyles'." They made quotes around the words with their fingers.

"That must be hard, for everyone," Celia said. The waiter was returning with their food. Denver picked up their toast and started to slather it with butter from those little plastic containers with the foil lids.

"Yeah, it's not easy. I mean, I'm not even really 'out' at work," Denver admitted softly. "But work isn't the same, it's not family. Family feels like it can stick to you, you know?"

"Oh yeah," Celia said. She had picked up the salt and was dumping an obscene amount of it on her eggs, followed by entirely too much pepper for Denver's comfort. "I've been pretty lucky with my family. I can tell being queer makes them uncomfortable, and they don't want me to be too public about it, but they don't get to make that choice for me now that I don't live close to home. I want to be my most authentic self, and they don't get to dictate what that is for me."

"True," Denver said. They looked towards the door where Tate had disappeared. "I guess that's why I'm on them a bit about saving. I think they miss living in a city too much, like a big one, that's further away from their family. I hope this is the year they're comfortable with moving away."

Celia chewed thoughtfully, although Denver could not understand how she managed to put eggs with that much salt in her mouth and they were pretty sure they could hear her teeth crunching through it. But her eyes were soft, drawing them in with her sincerity. "You'll miss them. But you'll be happy for them."

"True," Denver repeated. They sighed. "They might be my best friend. But I'll still have Quita and Jesse. I don't think they'll ever leave Quaint City."

"What about you?" Celia asked. Denver smiled at her.

"I'm open to any and all possibilities," they said diplomatically.

Celia nodded and gave a happy wiggle. "Okay. Back to the subject at hand. Plants?"

Denver snickered. "Absolutely not. I would kill them and that doesn't seem fair."

"You might not kill them. Plants are very reactive. If you were unhappy in a previous living situation, you probably were focused on self-care instead of plant care," Celia said. She shoved another bite of eggs in her mouth before she could giggle.

Denver smirked. "You really believe that?"

"I do... not," Celia said, giving a shrug. "But nothing else is working so it can't hurt, right?" She had a valid point there.

"I love plants," Denver said honestly, pushing their soggy chipped beef with toast around their plate. It had seemed appealing when they ordered it, but between the guilt over job-shaming Tate and the flock of butterflies that had settled somewhere in their heart region, they were less hungry now. "But I'm more of a botanical garden type person than a 'living things in my home that I'm responsible for' kind of person."

"No kids, then," Celia said, and Denver couldn't tell if it was a question or not.

"Nah. I mean, I never really wanted them but I think if Erin had asked I might have considered it. It's all really scary for me right now, though. I think the world is messed up and I'm just figuring out gender and stuff," Denver said quickly. "How could I have a kid?"

Celia nodded. "Fair. And good to know."

"How about you?" Denver asked.

"Oh, I love plants," Celia said with a wicked grin. There was a bit of butter and strawberry jelly at the corner of her mouth and Denver knew that even if they were allergic to strawberries, they'd have risked death and an epi-pen to taste it from that exact spot. "My apartment was full of them before I moved. I love taking care of things, if I'm being honest, but that probably won't include children without several miracles in the future."

Denver nodded, and the way that Celia's eyes were shiny, they knew it was a touchy subject for her. They didn't know if they should press or back off, so they managed a, "That's apparent."

Celia frowned. "What?"

"The way you care about things," Denver said quietly. "You took care of me today, after having barely even met me. And the way you handled Tate was amazing. You give a lot."

Celia's lips were twitching their way up again. "That's true. I never really looked at it that way."

Denver tilted their head to the side. "What way did you mean it?"

"I just saw a really cute person and I wanted to spend time with them, making them feel good. If that involves shopping for home decor, a passion of mine, well, gosh, I'll just have to suffer," Celia said softly, and there was a vivid warmth in her eyes. Her tongue darted out to lick the corner of her mouth, seeking that spot of strawberry. Denver swallowed.

"Thanks," they managed weakly. "You're- You're pretty cute."

Celia winked. "I know."

Lunch was full of stupid little things that made Denver's heart sing. Things like footsies under the chrome-edged table and rubbing their legs together for quick moments that seemed electric. They'd forgotten love could be like this. Denver paused in the shameless flirting to glance up at Tate when they were heading out the door from their interview. Tate nodded back but didn't come to say hi. Denver was going to have to text them later to see how everything had gone. And maybe to say sorry for being such a hardass. Following lunch, Denver and Celia piled back in her packed truck and drove to Denver's apartment. They remembered moving in with Erin, and how in her organized, efficient way she had made Denver and their friends do a lot of the heavy lifting while she stayed in the apartment and dictated where things went and how they were displayed.

That was a valid way of doing things, and Denver didn't think negatively of the experience except that Erin had come off as kind of 'too good to work' instead of genuinely concerned with organizing their living space.

Alternatively, Celia was insistent on unloading everything together and making trips up and down the stairs, letting Denver tell her where to put things. Not that Celia would dictate this apartment, she didn't live here, but at the same time she made a comforting show of letting Denver choose. That's all Denver really ever wanted, some actual say in how things worked. Maybe a little reassurance that their taste wasn't completely awful.

"We really put a lot in the truck, didn't we?" Celia asked, wiping sweat from her forehead and smearing her hands down her shirt. Denver nodded.

"Well, we were having fun," they said. Celia nodded. She stepped towards them, right into their space, and reached up to do the same for them. She brushed their damp bangs back out of their face, making sure none of their hair was stuck to their skin. She smiled.

"Are we still having fun?"

Denver stared down at her, lips parted. "Oh yeah."

"Good. Because we have to decorate this place. It's like if a saltine cracker were an apartment. And unsalted," Celia said, glancing around. Denver snorted, but their heart was racing. There had been a moment, there. A moment where someone cute, someone who knew they were nonbinary, had stepped into their space as though it was desirable to be close to them. It made them want to scrap all the projects and show Celia their...

mattress. Okay, maybe they did need to fix a few things before showing her the bedroom.

As it happened, the bedroom was the place she wanted to start.

Celia had called in a favor while they were in Blue Goat Township, which meant a pit stop at D.I.Y. warehouse. Together, they picked up a few discarded wooden palettes to create an industrial platform for Denver's mattress. It was a little mid-aughts, but they were on a budget and the wood was free, so Denver wasn't about to complain. Not to mention, it felt homey. Their mattress wasn't on the floor anymore, but it was still an unconventional bed situation, that was also plenty sturdy for extra-curricular activities. Not to mention, the books, which Denver hadn't remembered having, that Celia slotted into the gaps. It looked... charming. Cozy. Something the room hadn't been when Erin had lived there.

Celia hadn't been kidding about adding plants to the apartment, either. While Denver sanded down the palettes, she made this amazing draped garland of vines that went over one window with fake leaves she got at the dollar tree. From it, she wrapped little bottles with rough brown string and put tiny roses in them, hanging each bud lovingly amongst the greenery.

It wasn't redoing what Denver was already working with, it was *embellishing*, and Denver adored it.

With clean bed sheets added to the mattress, and the mattress stacked back on top of the palettes, they both flopped down and then rolled so they were facing each other. Celia's hair was a disaster, frizzing up a tiny bit from the heat and all the hard work, and Denver found it adorable. Together they'd picked some deep jewel toned throw pillows, and one of them must have been leftover from Halloween because there was a detailed skull on the front, and her cheek was smashed against it.

"The leaves and flowers, that's all something I learned during the initial lockdown," Celia told them softly. "At the time, my bedroom didn't really have any windows. So I went online and ordered all these fake plants. I mean, it was March when everything kicked off anyways, so there was no real greenery outside, but I was feeling so claustrophobic. I made a little fake garden, so it wasn't so bad until we were able to go outside."

That's really smart," Denver said, and they watched the beautiful blush that spread over Celia's nose and cheeks.

"Why, thank you," she said, and she batted her eyelashes playfully. "I pride myself on my almost-creativity."

"Almost? I'd say you're pretty darn creative," Denver told her. She grimaced.

"Some people haven't been so complimentary. My ex," she replied. "I remember this one time, I'd done a jacket up. Just a denim jacket, pretty basic, and I was painting with a stencil so it wasn't like *real* painting. My friend complimented me on it, and my ex just rolled his eyes and said, 'Creative? more like half-creative'. I never forgot that. I mean, it's not like I'm making real art."

"Who says you aren't? I mean, other than that guy," Denver said, quickly tacking on the last part. "Real art is just the act of making. I bet your ex wasn't so creative either."

"Oh, don't get me started. He wasn't crafty or anything, but some of the ideas he would come up with. You should've heard him and his 'bisexuality isn't real' argument. I don't know why I dated him," Celia said honestly. She scooched closer. "It doesn't bother you? If I mention my ex?"

It clicked suddenly for Denver that her ex had probably banned her from talking about other people within their relationship, and Denver's already soft heart bent further in her direction. They smiled in what they hoped was a reassuring manner. "Of course not. I want to know all about you. Besides, it sounds like your ex was a massive douchebag."

Celia wiggled closer, and Denver was shaken by how close she was now, how they could feel the heat radiating off her body. "Thank you."

She leaned in and pecked a soft, lingering kiss to Denver's cheek.

And then she rolled away.

"Come on! We have work to do!"

Denver groaned. Suddenly, they really did not feel like doing the work today.

CHAPTER FIVE

Denver worried they'd ordered too much pizza for dinner, but they wanted to give Celia a surprise for helping out all day, so they just went with two large pizzas and a twenty-four piece buffalo wing, and a two-liter of soda. If the two of them didn't finish it all, they'd have some leftovers for the next day or two, which was fine. The living room was coming along nicely, but Denver knew that they were going to need to pause. They'd started early and while Celia had a ton of energy, Denver was certainly not a teen anymore. Rest sounded good.

The subject of exes kept popping up. Probably because Celia would go to move something or ask Denver's opinion of something, and a look would cross their face as they remembered how said item got to that particular spot in the first place. Then, she would gently squeeze their hand, and remind them that both of their exes sounded terrible.

"Everyone has a terrible ex. I know this one girl, Scarlett, who started a sewing business during the pandemic," Denver said. They folded a black patterned throw blanket that they'd picked up at the thrift store for a few bucks because it looked cozy and draped it over the back of the sofa. "Her ex called her fat in front of her roommate and then proceeded to tell her that all the clothes she'd been making were ugly muumuus. First of all, they were babydoll dresses-"

"And there's nothing wrong with muumuus. I don't know why people think they're so ugly," Celia interrupted. She was smoothing over a large panel of removable sticker wallpaper, which had changed one of the beige walls into a deep emerald statement wall.

"Also true! And her style, it's like a Courtney Love caftan situation," Denver said. "You'd probably love her stuff. Some of it is made from old sheets and has cartoons printed all over."

"But again, what's wrong with caftans? I have some. I wear them around the house. They're comfortable," Celia objected. She finished with the wallpaper and stood back, with her hands on her hips, to admire her work. "Sometimes you just don't need a waistband around your stomach, judging you."

"You're right," Denver agreed. They stepped up behind her and looked at the wall. "This is a gorgeous color."

"You picked it!"

Yeah, but it was your idea, and you helped put it up, so I think you should get some of the credit," Denver told her. She laughed.

"I'll take it. But seriously, I don't understand why people hate comfort, or hate other people being comfortable. It's not an insult to you if someone wants to wear something. Like your boots," Celia continued, still on the subject of Scarlett's dresses. "You wear those heavy boots, but I know a lot of people who wouldn't want to wear them. That doesn't mean you should stop."

She paused, and she chewed on her lip as she thought about the entire situation. "What happened to Scarlett?"

Denver grinned and gave her a wink. "Her roommate kicked the boyfriend out, threatened to call the cops and then they started dating. Kam is a really sweet girl and she makes Scarlett very happy."

Celia's frown turned into a beaming smile. "Excellent."

"And you're absolutely right. There is nothing wrong or ugly or negative with being comfortable," Denver said quietly. They thought about their recent coming out, and their group of trans friends who were also in varying stages of realizing their true selves. "There's nothing wrong with being your authentic self."

"Your ex again?" Celia asked, and Denver nodded. She reached up to cup Denver's face, cradling it in her hands like it was a precious thing. "If you changed for her, you're not being you. And I like you. I'm glad you're you."

"I'm glad you're you, too," Denver replied. Their phone buzzed, and they broke contact with Celia to see that their dinner had arrived. "Ah! I hope you're hungry. I got pizza. A lot of it."

Celia giggled. "I love pizza."

"Awesome," Denver said. By the time they returned to the apartment with the boxes in hand, Celia had pulled out plates and napkins. She'd set two places on the coffee table and lit a little candle in the middle.

"Romantic, like a date," she said with a shy smile. Denver grinned. "You don't mind eating on the coffee table? I figured we could watch a movie or something, if you're not sick of me yet."

Denver stopped themselves from admitting they didn't think they could ever get sick of Celia and just set the boxes down before pulling Celia in for a hug. "Thanks. I am definitely up for a movie with you."

She hugged them back, letting their bodies sway. "Thank you for dinner."

Denver would never be able to remember the movie that they chose. They were on their newly cozy-fied sofa, sitting next to a pretty girl, eating pizza and getting to know one another as whatever they'd landed on for viewing played in the background, entirely ignored.

"Did I ask you what you did for work earlier?" Celia asked, happily sucking the meat off of a chicken wing that had been dipped in a puddle of ranch dressing. "I can't remember."

"It's okay, it's not very memorable until you have a technology issue. I'm in I.T. I basically fix computer issues for this company, it's really boring. It's okay, I mean. It pays the bills and I can work remotely during all the stuff going on, because I can just hop into people's machines to troubleshoot. It helps me, um, stay private about my other stuff, too. The non-binary stuff," Denver said with a sigh. "I wanted to be a drummer, but I was born without a sense of rhythm."

Celia licked her fingers and sat her plate down on the table. She grabbed a napkin to dry off her digits and pulled Denver to their feet. "I cannot believe you don't have rhythm. Come on, everyone has rhythm."

She tugged them around the coffee table and started to wriggle her hips. "Come on, show me your moves."

Denver flushed. It was a little uncomfortable. There wasn't any music, just the movie, and yet somehow watching Celia's hips move back and forth, the round curves of them bouncing and swaying, well. That was certainly a sight to see. "I don't know-"

"Am I making you uncomfortable?" Celia asked. She seemed sincere. She'd stopped dancing and looked at them with concern in her eyes.

"Nn-No, no, not much," Denver asked. They wondered how red their cheeks were because they felt hot all over. "I just, I think I'm more of a slow dancer."

Celia frowned for a moment, but then her expression cleared. She reached for Denver's hands, placing them on her soft hips. Denver couldn't help but squeeze a little, feeling her softness yielding under their hands. She looped her arms around their neck and lined her body closer to theirs. "Is this okay?"

"Yeah," they whispered. She started the motion, leading them into a gentle sway, back and forth, to no music at all.

"So, you don't want to do I.T.?" she prompted.

"I think it's just that sometimes I wish I were doing something more creative. But I'm not an artist, like my friend Scarlett, or you," Denver said softly. "I've never been the artsy type until this week, to be honest."

"Aren't you the one that just said there's a lot of ways to make art?" Celia replied. Her voice was quiet, and gentle. "I think you're more creative than you believe."

"Nah. I mean, you're the one that helped with all this. I probably would have never come up with any of these ideas," Denver replied. They were lost in her eyes.

"Art is whatever you want it to be. You don't have to live it all the time," Celia replied. "I get looked down on for my job, you know."

"Really?"

"Oh, yeah, because I'm in my thirties and I'm not a manager, I'm just a clerk in a box store. My mom is on my ass a lot about that. But, you know, I understand it better." Celia paused and nibbled her lip in that nervous way she had. "I can come off as pretty confident but I can also miss a lot of social cues. I would have a difficult time navigating office politics. It sounds like torture, if I'm being honest. If I had a nine-to-five, I think I'd cry. I don't like capitalism, but I can understand transactions well enough."

Denver considered that, tilting their head to the side. "Was I a transaction?"

The two of them had stopped shuffling, but Celia was still clinging to Denver's shoulders. "You were beautiful. I knew that I'd regret not meeting you."

"That's a bit woo-woo," Denver pointed out. Celia smiled.

"I think you need more woo-woo in your life," she replied. They grinned.

"You're not wrong."

They switched arms, then, and Denver felt something shifting between them. Celia moved her hands from where they were linked behind Denver's neck, bringing them down over Denver's sides. Her touch was firm, so as not to tickle, and with intent. Her body was warm and firm where she was pressed against them. Denver's own hands came up to drape over her shoulders and they cupped the back of her head, gazing into her eyes.

"I'd like to kiss you," they said. She grinned.

"I'd like to kiss you, too," Celia replied. She leaned in and pressed her lips against Denver's, who then gave an appreciative little moan and tipped further in. Celia's lips opened, allowing Denver's tongue to slip into the warm, wet slide of her mouth, her tongue against theirs. After a few minutes of the sweetest kissing, Celia pulled back to look at them.

"I'd like to do more with you, too," she whispered. Her lips were a bare, small space away from Denver's, and they could feel the ghost of breath against their mouth. She swallowed heavily, and when her eyes met Denver's, her pupils were like large black moons against the hazel of her irises. "If that's okay?"

"It's- It's *more* than okay," Denver said softly. Celia blushed.

"I need to know where," she broke off as Denver pecked small kisses to her cheeks, and along her jawline. "Where you'd like me to touch you?"

The real question on her lips, the one she wasn't quite asking, was one that Denver appreciated enormously. Their heart soared at the realization. She was asking about Denver's body and their complicated relationship with gender. Was it okay to touch or would she trigger Denver's mind to have a complete panic attack, or trigger dysphoria. No one had ever thought to ask, although, to be fair, Denver had only recently come out, but the level of care that Celia was showing them seemed almost too good to be true. In reality, it was just an act of what should be common decency and talking about consent with a partner, but as no one had ever asked, this seemed so new, so sweet, that Denver's chest clenched tightly. They licked their lips.

"I'm alright with being touched everywhere you want to touch. My body," Denver said, and they pressed forward meaningfully, pulling her even more flush against them, "is more than willing to be explored. But, if I'm being honest, I'd rather touch you."

Celia's smile was excited while managing to be indulgent. "Are you sure?"

"Maybe I'm discovering I'm a bit of a service top, maybe I just find you so attractive that I just can't stand not touching you. Either way, we could find out together," Denver whispered. Celia didn't answer in words. She surged up and kissed Denver again. It was thankful, then it was worshipful, and then it was demanding.

"Sofa?" she panted once they resurfaced for air. Her hands were now firmly gripping Denver's ass through their clothes, squeezing appreciatively as though she were appraising a peach before purchasing.

"Bed?" Denver asked, a bashful tone taking over. "Maybe christen the new sheets? Celebrate our job well done?"

"I keep telling you, you did more on your own than you think you did. I just helped," Celia said. Denver silenced her with another sweet peck.

"Tell me some more," Denver said playfully, giving her a wink. "Tell me all kinds of things."

Celia's lips twitched, her eyes heating up at the suggestion, the subtext that was etched in that request. "Take me to your bedroom, then."

There was definitely tripping as Denver attempted to pull them both towards the bedroom. There was a good few minutes spent paused, Celia having pressed Denver against a wall and pinned them there with her hands, her clever, creative, talented hands, hard enough to tip one of the new pieces of art to the floor. Denver moaned appreciatively as she pulled their shirt over their head and laved her tongue over their nipple. She brought one of Denver's hands up to cup her through her bra, encouraging to squeeze the handful of tempting flesh they found there.

"I'm not a fan of nipple stuff, but I do love having them massaged," she said before running her tongue from Denver's jaw down to their collar bone. They continued to squeeze, to lift and appreciate what they found there. "That okay?"

"Perfect," Denver answered, crushing their mouths together again. They pulled back and added, "I liked the way you, um. Did the same…?"

Celia's answering grin was positively mischevious. Her hands were on Denver's bum in less than a second, rolling the small but pert flesh she found there. "Like this, do you?"

Denver was too busy pressing kisses to her cheeks, her lips, the tip of her nose. The flat, hard strength of the wall behind them, the warm, softness of her body in front of them. They reached for the button on her jeans, hesitating with open eyes, asking the question without any words. She nodded, and

Denver's fingers flipped the button open before pulling the zipper down. They made a show of it, just a little. Wriggling the denim over the lushness of her hips, her ass, before tugging the pants down gently over her thighs. Appreciating those thighs as they were revealed to them. Celia gasped as her underwear followed, hooked on Denver's fingers and pulled, teased down off of her.

"Gosh," she breathed. Denver snickered, and raised an eyebrow.

"Gosh?" they asked. She nodded. Denver noticed that she was braced above them, with her hands supporting her against the wall. They licked their lips.

"Are we sure the bed is the goal?" they asked. They tilted forward and left a meaningful kiss against her thigh, so close to the inner thigh. Celia trembled and Denver's heart sped up, hammering in their chest. "This seems to be working so well for us."

"Well, since you asked, this is definitely working well," Celia said. She whimpered as Denver pressed another meaningful kiss to her other thigh, sucking a bit of the flesh into their mouth and rolling it gently. "Working super well for me."

This close, Denver could smell. Could practically taste. They licked a stripe, slow and hot, along her inner thigh, feeling that tremble again. Were her thighs sensitive? Were they going to be doing this long enough for Denver to find out? A small bite revealed another shiver and an appreciative moan. Denver looked up at Celia, knowing that the want must be apparent on their face. "Still good?"

"Oh, God, don't stop," Celia said, ending her plea with a sweet, breathless giggle. One hand left the wall and ran through Denver's hair. "Please."

"Since you asked so nicely," Denver said with a cheeky smile.

Their mouth still wanted to taste and explore that supple flesh. Celia's thighs were a gift that they wanted to fully take advantage of. As their mouth worked over her skin, leaving behind little lovebites and marks that would bloom into hickeys, their fingers delved into other territory. With one hand firmly on her hip, helping to hold her in place as her fingers were still stroking Denver's hair, maybe even tugging from time to time, Denver's fingers were finding the slick promise nestled in soft, folded skin. Denver's fingers moved teasingly along the outside, feeling just a hint of moisture, before their fingers spread out, pressing down and outlining the shape of her. She whimpered again.

"Good?" Denver asked quietly.

"Never better," Celia promised.

Denver sucked another hard mark to her inner thigh, enjoying the shudder and tremble of her body, and then set to work with their tongue. With every drag of their tongue against her slick folds, they felt her brace harder against the wall. Her hand paused in its stroking as Denver's fingers joined their tongue, slipping inside to stroke and tease. Celia, between those tantalizing noises she was making, would direct them.

"Forward," she'd gasp. "Harder. Suck-"

Denver did everything she asked. Their tongue laved over that most sensitive spot, following the gentle, barely-there rocking of Celia's hips. Her walls started to flutter around their fingers, to suggest that she was working closer and closer to release. Denver continued to lick and suck until the moment when they were sure she was on the verge. With one final, firm crook of their fingers, they sucked in hard and pressed their tongue against the spot where she was directing them. With the hand that wasn't inside of her, they pressed firmly on the skin above her pelvic bone, giving pressure where they knew it was needed.

The sounds Celia made were incandescent. She sobbed and fell forward against the wall, letting her forehead rest on her crossed arms. Her breaths came in shallow pants.

Denver grinned up at her. "Okay?"

She gave a breathless laugh as she stared down at them. "Fantastic."

Denver's grin brighted. "Excellent. Bed?"

Celia laughed again and then helped Denver up off their knees. "Come on. Let's do that again."

Denver smiled and knew that they would love to do *that*, every night, probably until the end of creation. Or whatever else Celia could come up with.

CHAPTER SIX

Denver wasn't a morning person, but then again, they weren't used to having someone in their bed with them. Erin had been someone who liked to get up early and do things like morning runs or gym workouts. Not that there was anything wrong with that, but it meant that she didn't linger for cuddling. Towards the end of their relationship, Denver would allow themselves to pass out on the sofa late at night in order to avoid going into the bedroom and potentially waking up Erin. They became real friendly with late night ads and three a.m. infomercials. Now, as Denver slowly regained consciousness, with the morning light casting interesting shadows through their new vine curtains, they realized that they weren't alone.

Celia was pressed close behind them, with her arm draped solidly around Denver's waist, and her nose buried into the space behind their shoulder blades. Denver wasn't used to being the 'little spoon', and they found it quite nice. Still, they wanted to turn over and look at her. She'd been so responsive the night before, so warm and open, they wanted to watch her sleep and bask in the gift that was Celia. She'd allowed Denver to play her like an instrument, and at the end Denver had allowed her to take them in hand and make her own sort of art with their body. They'd both been thoroughly wrung out and breathless before it was all said and done.

Denver twisted their body to look at her.

She was too fricking adorable.

The way the morning light and the shadows of the leaves danced across her face, the way her eyelashes rested against the roundness of her cheek. The very tiny, unmistakable snore that snuck out of her nose. It was all precious. Denver was well on their way to being entirely smitten.

Celia was probably going to be hungry, Denver thought. They certainly were.

They slipped quietly out of bed to do something about that. The bathroom was first, for morning reasons, and as they brushed their teeth they looked around at the room. It was as plain as the rest of the apartment had been, but now instead of being sad about it, they saw the potential. The hope that this space was truly going to start reflecting the person they wanted to be. Black walls would probably be too much for such a tiny bathroom, but what about a dark gray? Would that make it cozy? Did that sticker wallpaper hold up in a steamy environment?

Denver smiled. They were certainly going to find out.

As they stepped into the living room on their way to the kitchen, they took in the work of the night before. Near the window, wedged against the wall, was a little bistro table and chairs. It was one of those round, metal outdoor tables which had been on clearance since summer was coming to an end. Bought for a song. But it gave rock and roll, metal vibes and Denver loved it. There was a little black vase with flowers in the center. Denver took in the artwork that Tate had watched them create, the green statement wall, the large (fake) potted plant in the corner, and the throw pillows. It all felt so much like home.

With a happy sigh, Denver moved to more important questions what should they have for breakfast?

As they were starting the coffee to brew, there was a knock on the door. Denver rolled their eyes. Tate or Jesse, probably, and Denver was going to have to admit to them why they couldn't come in. Denver knew they'd never hear the end of the teasing. Maybe they could make something up. Paint fumes? Denver opened the front door.

The breath felt like it had been knocked out of them. "Erin?"

"Hi, Denver," Erin said, her lips pulling into a familiar smile that Denver would've killed to see just a few short weeks ago. She held up two cups of coffee from Devil's, Denver could tell by the logo. They couldn't imagine that had been easy on her. In the break-up, Denver had definitely gotten all the friends at Devil's Stomping Grounds. "Do you have a second? I'd like to talk."

Denver crossed their arms over their chest. They hated how they felt like they were in trouble, like they'd somehow been cheating on Erin, which was ridiculous considering they'd been broken up. Still, getting caught with a new... something by the person you had previously been sleeping with was awkward to say the least. Denver shook their head. "Now isn't a good time."

"Oh, that's a shame. Jesse said-"

Denver's eyes flashed. "Jesse? Jesse said what?"

"Can't I come in?" Erin asked. Her smile faltered. "We could talk. Maybe we could even get some breakfast."

"She can come in," Celia said from behind Denver. Denver looked over their shoulder at her, and their breath caught. She looked so good in the morning light. Her rumpled shirt, her paint-covered jeans. Even the way her hair was falling out of the fluffy bun she'd pulled it into. "I have to go and get ready for work."

"You don't have to go," Denver said, but Celia had already put on her shoes and had her bag in hand. She patted them on the arm as she passed.

"No, it's fine. See you later, Denver," Celia said. Denver tried to understand the expression on her face, but they couldn't quite nail it down. It wasn't angry, but it wasn't sad, either. They should've run after her, begged her to go out to breakfast with them and pretend Erin hadn't just ruined one of the nicest things that had happened to Denver in a long time. Sadly, Erin stood in the way with an expectant look on her face. Denver wanted to scream.

"What are you doing here, Erin?" they asked. Erin pushed inside, but she stopped almost immediately when she started to realize how much had changed since she'd been gone.

"Oh wow, Denver. This is amazing," she breathed. It was, Denver knew that, but as the words left her mouth, their stomach soured. After all the times she'd denied them the opportunity to put their stamp on the apartment, after all the times she'd complained about their preference for dark stuff, she came in and decided *now* that it was 'amazing'? Denver wanted to snap something.

"It is?"

"Oh, yeah, this is definitely you all over. It looks awesome. Chic, even," Erin said. Denver's frown only deepened.

"But you hate stuff like this," Denver said, trying to remain gentle in the face of all the hurt she had caused.

"I think hate is a strong word. Besides, it's grown-up. It looks like an adult lives here, not some kid. It's not a lot of metal posters," Erin pointed out. Oh, yeah, that was something Denver should do. They needed to get poster frames for the posters currently rolled and tucked into their closet. "This is the perfectly adult version of you."

Denver wanted to stamp their feet just on principle. "What do you want Erin?"

"It's hard to say, but I honestly wanted to apologize to you," she said. She offered the coffee again and this time Denver took it. It was hot, which was just horrendous in this weather, but they knew Erin drank hot coffee year round so it probably never occurred to her to get it iced. Just another way she only thought of herself and not the person she was trying to connect with. "I have some news."

"You're pregnant?" Denver guessed, joking at first but then wondering if that's why she was here. "Wait, you're not, are you? Because-"

"No! Oh, God, no," Erin said, and she gave a nervous laugh. "No, you're um, totally safe on that end of things. I'm queer. And I wanted you to know."

Denver's brain shut down completely. After all the - "What? When did you decide that?"

"I discovered that around the time we broke up," Erin started but Denver interrupted her.

"You broke up with me."

"After we parted," Erin said, her eyes flashing with

annoyance, "I started seeing a therapist over in Wintervale and we had a long talk about how I treated you after you came out. And it turns out that I might not be super straight myself. I'm- well, I mean, I think I'm bisexual. Actually, I think I'm also poly and I need to work harder on communicating my needs in a relationship because if I'd just told you how I was feeling, maybe…"

She didn't finish the sentence, which Denver was glad of. Denver didn't want there to be any doubt that they were broken up. The Denver from a month ago might have wavered, might have agreed to couples counseling, but this Denver had been left alone to think about things they wanted and how Erin had hurt them. This Denver had been introduced to Celia, who had helped show them potential in themselves. And Celia had left today thinking that Erin was back and probably that Denver was going to throw her away.

Unacceptable.

"So, anyway, I wanted to apologize. I realize that coming out at our age was a very brave thing and I should have been more accepting of you," Erin was saying. Denver's heart squeezed in their chest.

"Well, congratulations on coming out yourself. Now, please, get out of my apartment."

Erin's face fell. "Don't you want to talk?"

"Fuck no," Denver said, letting a growl edge into their words. They were getting pissed now, truly angry. "You played too many games. I literally don't care what you've decided or how it's affected you. You don't get some happy closure with me, Erin. At least, not right now."

Erin brushed her hair back from her forehead, a gesture she always did when she was getting annoyed at them. "Denver-"

"No, I mean it. Get out," Denver snapped. "You came over here, ruined a perfectly nice morning. You don't even think about things, do you? Do you even think about what kind of coffee I like or how constantly hearing you nag at me makes me question every fucking thing I know about myself? I'm working on being happy, without you, and I'd like you to go do the same somewhere else. Please, leave. Get out. I don't want to talk to you anymore."

She looked frustrated, and sad, but whatever she wanted to say stayed sealed behind her teeth. "Fine. Maybe, with some time-"

"Doubtful. And if you're thinking about fucking around with Jesse, that's between you. Don't drag me into it," Denver said. They pointed towards the door. "Get out."

Erin huffed but she nodded. "Fine. Since you can't be reasoned with. See you around."

Denver slammed the door behind her and twisted the lock as loudly and firmly as they could. "Unlikely."

They took out their phone and texted for back-up. They needed their friends, their family, to help them process what the fuck just happened.

"What the actual fuck were you thinking?" Tate groaned, leaning forward on their knees. Jesse and Tate were seated on Denver's sofa, while Denver was sitting on the floor, legs in criss-cross-applesauce formation. They looked around Denver's recently renovated apartment. "She comes here, she does all this stupid craft stuff with you-"

"I thought you liked craft stuff?" Jesse asked.

"That's besides the point. In this circumstance, it can be stupid," Tate said snappishly. "This cute girl who is absolutely new to town comes here and she sacrifices an entire Saturday during the plague to help you forget your old girlfriend and when Erin shows up, what do you do? Abandon her? Ask her to leave? I'd be pissed, too."

"It's not that bad," Jesse said.

"You only think that because you have a massive crush on Erin," Tate replied. Their face twisted with horror, as if they couldn't believe what had just popped out.

"You what?" Denver asked, turning on Jesse.

"Secret crush," Jesse said. "Besides, Quita would kill me dead."

"Well, yeah, of course she would. It's kind of cheating," Tate said. "And Erin fucking sucks."

"Actually," Jesse started, straightening up in his seat. "It's not cheating. We're talking about opening up the relationship, a bit. She loves me, and I want to marry her, but love doesn't just get used up. It's an endless-"

"Spare me," Tate said. "Love is for lonely people."

"Oh, so you," Jesse snarked back.

"Besides, Erin is kind of terfy," Denver said. "I mean, yeah, she cheated but there was also a 'if you weren't nonbinary, I wouldn't have to do this' kind of thing. There was a lot about- and hey, how do you even go from liking someone like Quita to someone like Erin?"

Tate lifted their eyebrows in agreement, giving Jesse the most pointed look they could before deciding it was time to rustle around in Denver's kitchen like some unwanted pest. Actually, Tate would make a good raccoon.

"How do you go from liking someone like Erin to someone like Celia?" Jesse countered. "*They're* not similar."

"Yeah, but Quita is so cool and chill, and Erin is just an uptight bag," Denver said quickly, but they wondered if Jesse had a point.

"Erin *is* an uptight bag. Celia *is* cool and chill," Jesse said confidently.

"I hate when you're right," Denver mumbled. "And for the record-"

"Yeah, yeah, I know, you were talking about how I love a barista versus how I wanna bone a terfy lawyer, but I'm glad you recognize how that sounded," Jesse said. "And Erin clearly wants to try changing. I mean, why else did she come here?"

"I guess." Denver ran their fingers through their hair. "One week ago I had sworn off dating drama for forever. Now here I am wondering if this girl I've only known for a week might be the love of my life and, even if she is, what should I do because I'm pretty sure I've already blown my shot." They looked up at Tate, who was shoving a mug of coffee under their nose. "Thanks."

"Don't tell anyone I'm nice to you. I'll deny it," Tate replied.

"No one would believe me, anyway. What should I do?" Denver asked. "Celia isn't like anyone I've ever known. We-"

"Had mindblowing sex? Probably on this very sofa?" Tate asked as they flopped down again, wiggling their butt against the cushions as if they enjoyed the idea of that thought.

"Don't be disgusting," Denver groaned. Tate cackled.

"What can I say, it's a gift," Tate said. "My brother in Christ, as the kids would say ironically, please go and talk to her. Like, where is she today? Text her. Talking is like, the number one thing, isn't it?"

"Talking and establishing boundaries. If you can effectively do that, in theory, you can make almost any relationship work," Jesse said. He grinned. "At least, that's what I tell myself with Qui."

"She must really love you to be as patient as she is with your dumb ass," Tate said, but when they looked over at Jesse, it was clear that they were very, very fond of him and probably just as protective as Quita.

"One day, Tate, you are going to fall ass over tin cup for someone, and I'm going to laugh my butt off," Jesse threatened. "How are you a romance writer without a freaking romantic bone in your body?"

"It's easy," Tate said. "It's like being a scientist. I've got my magnifying glass and I'm just watching all the ants roast in the sun."

"I really don't think that is being a scientist," Denver mumbled. "Okay, all of you out. Get out of my apartment. I need to work on this."

"You are literally no fun," Tate complained, and pretended to be hurt with Denver shoved at them. "We're going, we're going. Beau is going to be so pissed. I told her she'd have the apartment to herself today."

"Too bad, so sad," Denver quipped.

"Come on, Tate. Quita is at the cafe. We can go bother her," Jesse said, pulling Tate along.

"Don't you ever get sick of her?" Tate complained, even though Tate never got sick of Quita.

"Absolutely not," Jesse grinned. He waved at Denver as he pushed Tate out the door and closed it behind them.

Denver felt restless. They felt like a buzzing of bees fluttering up in their chest, and the sleepless night they had caused their eyes to sag. They stood and wandered around the room, touching the things that Celia had helped them put there. Even though they'd only known each other a short time, it really did feel like Celia had stamped her mark on here, like some part of this now belonged to her instead of to Erin.

Denver was really going to need to find a therapist. It was probably not healthy to continually hand over their space to other people. But Celia had been there, and her little thumbprints lingered over every project, every new piece of furniture.

They went into their bedroom and slid off their plain jeans, pushing the t-shirt they had worn over their head. They were due for a shave soon, the bits carved out by their ears looking a bit sloppy. That was the problem with style. Once you decided to have it, it required constant upkeep. Denver looked at their naked body in the mirror. They felt indifferent to what they saw, which might have been what took them so long to realize that they were non-binary. Other people had more severe dysphoria, maybe. Other people hated what they saw when they looked in the mirror. Denver just didn't care. That wasn't where their identity stemmed from.

They opened their closet and removed the outfit that Celia had chosen from the thrift store. They had some work to do.

CHAPTER SEVEN

The drive to Blue Goat Township wasn't long enough. As insane as last Sunday had felt, taking that first step out into the world, this Sunday was mild. There was no traffic as Denver drove along the winding creek road. The smooth pavement of tourist-friendly Quaint City started to blend into the pothole marked road of Blue Goat. Historic houses started to space out, becoming ranchers that had been built in a more recent century and box stores started looming. What a strange and liminal place the outskirts of small towns could be. There the charm started to fall away to the necessity, aesthetic giving over to practicality.

They hoped like hell that Celia was actually working. It had seemed too creepy to go by her house, and she said that she had a shift today. Did she want Denver there? Could she be so mad that Erin had showed up without any warning? It wasn't like it was Denver's fault.

All the same, they had done a quick online search for the D.I.Y. Warehouse store hours, figured out the closing time, and went through the drive-through of the nearest chain place. Denver hadn't seen Celia in just over eight hours, but it still felt too long. They were quickly realizing that Celia was a person they might never get sick of seeing. They wanted more with Celia. They wanted to take her to dinner and ask about her life. They wanted to curl on the sofa with her and watch bad movies that ended in long, slow kisses. They wanted so many more nights like the one before, where they could watch her gasp and moan and clench. Where they could lick the sweat off her skin and taste her. And they didn't want it all now. They wanted it slowly. Torturously slowly, if that's what Celia wanted. Denver knew that they were going to want it all with Celia in a way that hadn't felt right until this very second.

Would Celia propose to them, eventually?

These were the stupid, giddy thoughts that Denver had while they waited for Celia's shift to end. They knew she was in the store because that truck was unmistakable, right down to the "I brake for yard sales" sticker on the back. They leaned against their own car, which they later regretted because the humidity was back and they were sure it was doing frizzy things to their hair, and they waited for Celia to come outside.

There weren't many trees in the parking lot, which allowed for a wide view of the sky. It felt big, open. Exposed. Denver watched as colors shifted from orange to pink to purple as the sun set, knowing that the days were slowly getting shorter and winter would come soon. Would Celia be willing to build a snow person with them? Did she like cocoa?

"Hey," Denver said quietly as Celia approached them. They held out the iced coffee they had brought as a peace offering. "I hit the drive-through on my way over. Figured after the kind of shift I witnessed last Sunday, you might need the caffeine."

It felt different from when Erin had brought Denver coffee. This time, Denver knew how Celia took hers and made the effort to get it right.

"Hey," Celia said quietly. She took the coffee, which was hopefully a good sign, and twisted her sneaker against the pavement. She wouldn't meet their eyes.

"Are you okay?" Denver asked.

"I don't know. I thought-" Celia chewed on her lip, considering her words very carefully. "I thought you would, I don't know. If I didn't see you again, I figured you'd be coming here to tell me to back off. Honestly. I know that we're not like, together or anything, but I'd like to get to know you better. If Erin is back, though-"

"No! No, no, that's finished. Erin is over and has been for a long time," Denver said. They pushed off their car. God, this anxious little mess was the most precious thing that Denver had seen in a long time. "Look, Celia, Erin wants me to be something I'm not. Even if you hadn't been there, it would be over. I can't be different for her."

"What does she want?" Celia asked, but it sounded like she'd meant, 'how could she want anything else?'.

Denver shrugged. "I'm not even sure she knows. She's starting a journey that only she can figure out."

Celia's lips quirked. "That sounds a bit woo-woo."

"I'm learning to appreciate the woo," Denver said. "She still wants a boyfriend and girlfriend. She still sees these roles on the binary, I think. And I can't be that for her. I can't shove myself into a box for anyone. I'm not different from the person she fell in love with. I just use a more accurate label to describe myself, and she couldn't handle it. I've got to look out for my well-being, too, you know? If she can't see that I'm the same, that signals to me she didn't really like me in the first place. I was just filling a column for her."

"Loving the whole idea of you kind of thing?" Celia prompted. Denver nodded with a grim smile.

"Something like that."

"I'm sorry, it's just. Alright, I know I came onto you pretty quickly, but I don't do that. I'm not usually the assertive one," Celia said. Her cheeks flushed, as if she were embarrassed, and Denver wanted to kiss them. "And I'm not saying anything bad about people who do, but I also am not the type to sleep with someone on the first date. I really like you. All of you."

"You don't have to-"

"Hold on, I want to get this off my chest. My previous experience has taught me not to ask for the things I want. And I might never really get over that, but I need you to know," Celia said. "When I saw you, I *wanted*. I wanted real bad. And not a label or an outfit or a gender. I just want you."

The butterflies in Denver's stomach were growing quickly, turning into pterodactyls. "I want you, too."

"Okay." Celia looked up at them. "You can't just show up here in a sexy outfit and give me smoldering eyes and an iced coffee every time we have a fight, you know."

"Me? Moi?" Denver pointed at their chest and pretended to look over their shoulders. "I? I give the smoldering eyes?"

Celia grinned back at them. "You give the smoldering eyes."

"Oh, I will have to be much more careful. I will yield this new power responsibly," Denver said. Celia giggled.

"You better."

"So... we're seeing each other again?" Denver asked hopefully, because they were still not entirely sure.

"Of course we are. I hope we're seeing each other right now. I haven't eaten all day and I'm starving."

VANE ATTRACTION

CHAPTER ONE

For all that Vane was known to be the biggest bitch in Quaint City, she wasn't typically prone to acts of violence against other people, but right now she could very cheerfully choke her aunt with a hand-crafted pumpkin latte from Devil's Stomping Grounds. Said latte was currently sitting in the cup holder of the shitty car she'd been driving since college, entirely untouched, and getting colder by the minute. Under normal circumstances, autumn was Vane's favorite time to be in Quaint City. The sweet little tourist trap where she'd set up shop was particularly adorable as the trees that lined main street all started turning orange and that perfect golden light started streaming through the front windows of her salon. Autumn light might not be the best for photographing blonde clients who wanted no warmth in their hair, but luckily autumn also brought hoards of 'please make me brunette, I'm tired of summer highlights'. Maryland was known for its oppressively humid air which made you feel damn whenever you set foot outside in the summer, and it always took until the end of September for everything to cool off, but once it did there was an undefinable magic quality to the air that seemed to imply anything was possible.

Sadly, 'anything' was a broad category and it didn't always mean 'good'.

Gran was dead.

Vane slammed her hands against the steering wheel of her car, grinding her teeth together in a way that would probably trigger one of her migraines. She could be such a cunt and three-quarters when she had a migraine. Her eyes pricked with tears. She didn't want to cry. It had taken her exactly forty-five minutes to get her make-up perfect for her shift at the salon, *her* salon. She would absolutely *not* cry. To cry in the parking lot behind her salon would be humiliating and show a complete lack of self-control and be an utterly grotesque waste of product. She would *not* cry.

Gran was *dead*, though.

It shouldn't hurt this much. America, capitalist piece of shit country that it is, seemed to believe that there was no real importance in a grandparent dying. Corporate jobs give you one day off, if you're lucky, and definitely do not include any kind of pay. Vane had been in salons where a stylist had lost a parent and the manager was offended when the person had asked for more than one day to grieve.

In theory, owning her own salon should make Vane more sympathetic to herself. It's not every day that you find out the person who took you in when your parents didn't care enough to keep you died on social fucking media. But Vane was tough. She'd made it to almost forty without having to deal with any of these squishy feelings. If successful corporations could be that cold, then Vane should be able to cut this feeling off at the throat, to push it back into the dark recesses of her heartless chest, but she just couldn't. She couldn't stop the choking, biting, cringing sadness that was threatening to wreck her perfectly painted face. She let out a dry sob.

Cancer was a bitch.

Vane should have gone to see her more often. She should've spent more time with her, but Vane was busy trying to take care of herself while also trying to make Gran proud. When her aunt would call to update her, Vane would just push it off until the next week.

"Soon," she'd promised. "I'll come see you soon, okay?"

But then there was payroll to do or accounting to keep up with or advertising for the salon to consider and plan. She'd pushed off visiting, or kept her visits short, and then lockdown had happened and she'd been basically forbidden from coming over, anyway. Her aunt Tammy had been quiet, but Vane was so busy trying to navigate this shit-storm of a virus and keeping her doors open that, if she were being honest with herself, she'd never even noticed the lack of communication. She'd been cut off enough that Tammy hadn't even called when Gran died. Vane found out on social media.

Vane slammed her hands onto the wheel again for good measure.

She was the type of stylist who was perpetually late, but she'd been recently... *inspired*... to start showing up on time for her shifts. It definitely had nothing to do with the warm, talented new girl that had started a few months ago and who was quickly worming her little way into Vane's chest. Right where her heart was supposed to be. So what if Vane had started getting to the salon early to sit in the parking lot and think about what she was going to say to Hannah when she saw her? What if she sometimes braved the lines of people waiting for coffee at Devil's Stomping Grounds just to take Hannah a cocoa and see her smile? Vane was definitely not smitten. And up until very recently, she'd had a boyfriend! Ross. What a loser. Vane was just trying to be a good business owner. And, like any good business owner with a few free minutes in her car, she'd just finished uploading a picture of that gorgeous balayage, white highlights melting down from a dark root, to the shop's social page only to see the post from her aunt. It was marked two weeks ago.

Gran had died two weeks ago and no one had bothered to call her.

And she'd missed the funeral.

Anger bubbled up in her chest, overwhelming the grief that also lurked there, but not enough to choke out the guilt that she should have tried harder. With glassy eyes, Vane leaned her leather-clad elbow on the windowsill of her car and remembered Gran. Funny, wonderful Gran, who had taken her in after her parents had kicked her out when they'd found her wrapped around Molly, the head cheerleader at her school. Gran, who had given her a place to live while she finished high school and the fifteen-hundred hour tech program that ended in her getting her cosmetology license. Gran, who had advised her while she worked for some of the worst jerks in the industry until she had enough to get her shitty car, her shitty apartment and then her beautiful salon. In that order.

A loud, inward gasp of air from her own lungs surprised her enough to snap her out of it. No, no. She couldn't possibly think of that now. Not when she was due in for her shift and clients were waiting. Vane tilted her head back and stared at the hole-riddled upholstery of her ratty old car. The fabric was tearing away, exposing the foam and metal underneath. She blinked back the tears that threatened to spill over and breathed, in and out, to calm herself down. She should really replace this stupid thing, she thought. Her salon, her image, all relied on cohesive branding. Expensive, rebellious and tasteful, that was Vane. Stylish. Edgy. Vane's car didn't fit the image. Every cent she earned was poured back into the salon, leaving her with very little time or energy for herself.

Or Gran, if she wanted to be a bitch to herself about it.

She breathed out, letting a big whoosh of air escape her. She couldn't go into her salon like this. She couldn't face Bex and Hannah like this. She breathed in, sucking back a sob and forcing herself to be calm, and then whooshed out again. In and out. One foot in front of the other. She could get through today.

Vane grabbed her keys, and her black leather tote bag, and stepped out of her car.

And immediately tripped.

She made the mistake of catching herself with her hands, which sent her purse spilling onto the ground.

"Are you okay?"

Vane's head snapped up. Hannah was above her, with the back door of the salon propped open with a brick. She was wringing her hands together in worry before she bent down and started to pick up Vane's stuff off the ground. Her soft hand had just wrapped around Vane's cracked-screen phone when she made a little 'oh' sound. She gathered Vane's hands into her own and frowned. "Oh no, you're not okay."

Vane looked down. She swallowed. Her palms were cracked, scraped and bleeding, with little bits of gravel stuck to them. She swallowed again, because that stupid lump in her throat was refusing to go down. "I'm fine."

"Samantha, you're not fine."

Vane tried to cringe away from her, fingers curled in towards her wounds, but Hannah's grasp was too strong and she was trapped by those talented hands. "Vane."

Hannah sighed. "Samantha Vane. You are *not* fine."

Vane winced at her whole name being used. "I'll wear gloves today. It'll be fine. Why are you outside? Where's your mask?"

"Smoke break?" Hannah asked, and Vane pursed her lips, letting one perfectly blocked brow raise up in disbelief. Hannah deflated. As if Hannah would ever do something as tacky as *smoke.* "Alright, I was of course using the mask indoors, but Rebecca- errr, Bex- is doing some sort of video on layering polish and it's getting sort of toxic in there. It's such a nice day out, I thought maybe we should open the salon doors. And since my client is late anyway, I've been waiting outside. Taking advantage."

Hannah was adorable when she babbled, and she babbled when she was nervous, which was often. A blush was spreading over her round cheeks. Vane licked her lips. This time, when she pulled her hands back, Hannah let her take them.

It was a beautiful day. It was a perfect Fall day in Quaint fucking City. There was a cool breeze and warm sunshine and beautiful yellow and orange leaves on the trees. It was a perfect day and her grandmother was dead and her life was spilled out on the pavement of the sidewalk. Fan-fucking-tastic.

"Tell Bex she's only supposed to do toxic videos during closed hours. She needs to knock it off," Vane told her. She cleared her throat. "Let me just get my stuff and I'll be in."

Hannah seemed to know better than to argue, and Vane wondered if she'd been out there long enough to see her banging her fists against the wheel. Or, it could be Scott's influence. Hannah had come to Vane from a rival salon that gaslit it's employees and worked them all hours of the night and day. The owner, Scott Christian, could be entirely charming one minute and then with choice words eviscerate his assistants while all the clients and stylists watched in abject horror. The job had left marks on Hannah that Vane was trying her best to undo. Hannah went inside to warn Bex about Vane's mood, and Vane gathered up her life from where it lay on the pavement.

Vane was determined not to make a mess of herself or anyone else today. She picked up her phone, her case with her shears inside, and her planner, shoved them all back into her tote bag and picked herself up off the ground. She could do this. Gran would be disappointed in anything less.

As she entered the salon, Vane knew that she absolutely could *not* do this.

She held on for three clients. The first one was a standard full highlight, easy, she could do those in her sleep. While the highlight was processing, she didn't give herself time to think because she had a root touch-up on her favorite client, Bernadette, to apply while the highlight was working. She gave Bern a water and helped settle her in a chair by the large front window to wait while she finished the blow-out and haircut from the first highlight. She had bills to pay, a salon to keep running and Vane was certainly not going to give herself time to think about it.

She also kept sneaking glances across the salon at Hannah. Hannah was everything Vane wasn't. She was chubby where Vane was a thin slash of a person, she was shorter where Vane was tall and she had long, bleached out curls where Vane's own dark hair was a shorter shag. (Every bisexual needed a mullet in a pandemic year, right?) Where Vane was more inclined to frown or sulk, Hannah had a bright smile plastered on her face nearly all of the time. Probably because, at her old job, she would have been fired without one. Poor thing.

Today, more than once, she'd caught Hannah looking back at her. There was concern in her eyes and a constant question etching itself in the gentle lines between her eyebrows.

Vane was fine. She'd even argued with Bex about the nail polish, right? Couldn't be anything less than fine.

It all came to a head when, after a quick neck trim for a walk-in, Vane had blown out Bernadette's hair and was about to trim her bangs.

"Are you sure you're not going through something? Only people who are having mental collapses want bangs," Vane said to her as she sectioned off the front pieces of hair. Bernadette, the amazingly calm woman that she was, just shrugged.

"It's a pandemic year," Bern said. "Go nuts. It'll grow back." Vane frowned, not that Bernadette could see her lips turn downward behind her black mask. Vane sighed.

"I hate bangs," she muttered. "They're so easy to mess up. And they need constant trimming. I know I'm supposed to love bangs, 'cause you'll just have to come back and let me cut them over and over, but they suck. There's money in bangs. Bangs suck."

Bern kept her mouth shut and sucked on the straw of a melted iced coffee she'd gotten from Devil's during her processing time. It had been pretty funny watching the foil-headed woman with freshly painted toes, courtesy of Bex, splayed out with foam, toddling over to get a coffee. Vane had almost considered smiling.

As Vane drew herself up into a straightened position, elbows out and scissors poised to make the first cut on Bern's bangs, Bern let go of the straw, blinked her huge eyes at Vane and said, "Don't fuck it up."

Vane had been in this industry twenty years and she could count the number of complete fuck-ups she'd had on one hand.

But there it was. A hole, cut on the right side of Bernadette's fringe, mangling her haircut.

"Oh, *fuck*," Vane said. Her grip on reality was already shaking, but now she'd messed up her favorite client's hair, it was crumbling at the core. "Oh, ffffff- I'm so sorry!"

Bernadette waved her off. "It's not a problem. I screwed around and found out, hon, don't worry about it."

Vane's face was red. Especially considering Hannah was looking at her with wide eyes, clearly traumatized by what she'd just witness. Okay, maybe traumatized was a bit dramatic, but Vane accepted nothing short of perfection from the work Vane Attraction put out, and to have made such a rookie mistake-

Was it time to go home yet?

"I should have said no. I'm clearly not in the mood for bangs today," Vane said. She put her shears to work, point cutting in to try and blend the mess that one quick chop across Bern's hair had done.

"Yeah, I can tell," Bernadette replied. She watched Vane through her fringe with a curious gaze. "What's going on? You seem more tense than usual."

Ah, good. So Vane usually came across as tense and now it was worse. Vane cringed, making sure to pause her scissors this time. "I usually seem tense?"

Bern snorted. "Bitch, please. Are you joking? You're the epitome of tense. Intense, present tense, past tense. What's going on?"

Vane's eyes flicked to Hannah again, who was busy rolling a disgusting-smelling perm on a younger person with shaved sides. Hannah was engrossed enough in her work that Vane felt she could be honest with Bernadette. She huffed. And then she spilled. "My grandmother died."

Bernadette's eyes flew open wide and she gasped, making Hannah's head snap up from the roller she'd just settled. "Oh man! I am so sorry!"

"Shh, shh," Vane hissed. She shook her head at Hannah, hoping that she was conveying 'just get back to work' without looking too bitchy. She swallowed. "No, no, don't cry. If you cry, I'll cry, and I can't afford to cry, dude. I just need to get through today."

"Okay, but you know I've been coming to you for a long time. You're more than a stylist to me." Bern reached out to grip Vane's arm. "We're friends. If you need me, I'm here for you."

Vane nodded at Bernadette and she resumed trying to fix the

bangs. "Thanks, Bern."

In the end, she couldn't let Bernadette pay for the absolute disaster of a haircut, and Bern protested. Of course, the final cut wasn't so bad, but it wasn't what Bernadette had wanted and Vane was nothing if not a perfectionist, so she couldn't charge for it.

"You can't do that!" Bern objected. Vane waved her off.

"I'm the owner," Vane said in a gravelly voice that was getting too thick with unshed tears. "I can do what I want. Sorry I screwed up your bangs."

"Hey," Bern's voice dropped low and soft, even though she probably knew that doing so would set Vane off again. "If you need me, you have my number. I'm here for you."

Bern had lost her mother a few years ago, so Vane knew she would be more understanding than most, but she shook her head and said, "I'll call you if I need you. But I'm fine. I'll be okay."

Would she, though?

"It's a beautiful day outside," Hannah said brightly. She was walking up to the register with her client in tow, eyes beaming happiness at Vane. "Of course you'll be okay."

And, apparently, that was the straw that would break Vane's back. She broke down and started to sob uncontrollably. Bernadette wrapped her up in a hug that smelled of bleach and hairspray, swaying her from side to side.

"It's okay, girl. Let it all out," she murmured.

"What's wrong with Vane?" Bex asked from somewhere.

"I don't know," Hannah replied. Bernadette huffed against Vane's hair.

"You want me to tell them?" Bern asked her. It was all she could do to shake her head. She started to pull away, but Bernadette held her tight. "It's alright, Vane. This is normal, sweetie."

"I know," Vane wavered. "But not for me."

This time, she did pull back and wiped her cheeks where the tears had fallen. She looked around at her salon staff. "Death in the family. I'll be in my office."

She turned and fled, like the coward she was, leaving everyone else standing up front staring after her. She slammed the office door.

When she'd first moved into the retail space that held Vane Attraction, everything had been white and bland. She'd liked it, because it was a blank canvas that she could shape and mold into something really cool. Something different from other salons that she'd been to. And over the years, she'd made it her own, especially her office, because if she was going to have to spend time in there going over payroll and bills, she wanted it to feel like herself. She'd painted the walls a deep burgundy and she'd thrifted so many funky weird decorations, like the statue of an elephant dressed as the Virgin Mary or the throne that was her desk chair. It all came together in a creepy cool style that she was really proud of. Now, she was collapsed in the gaudy gold chair, feeling her chest constrict tighter and tighter as she tried not to cry, breathing in and out too heavily for her own good. Hyperventilating? Was she hyperventilating? All she knew was that the mask was sticking to her face and she was going to rip it off in like, five seconds, pandemic be damned.

There was a gentle knock on her door. "Vane?"

Fucking Hannah.

"Yeah?" Vane said, and she winced at how harsh she sounded. She really didn't want Hannah to think that she was as cruel as the last guy Hannah had worked for. She always swore if Scott Christian walked in front of her car she'd-

Well, she needed a new car, anyway.

Hannah opened the door and peered around the panel at Vane. Her eyes held nothing but concern. "Do you want me to call your other clients? I could ask them to move, or cancel. We can handle it without you if you'd like to go home."

Vane pinched the bridge of her nose and ground out, "I don't need to go home."

"Oh," Hannah said softly. Her brows pulled together. "Are you sure?"

"What would I do at home? Cry?" Vane pointed at her ruined

face. "I'm already doing that."

Hannah rolled her eyes. "Yes, I just thought you might not like to do it on your client's heads."

"I'm not going to cry." The itching behind Vane's nose told her otherwise but it's not like Hannah had to know that. "I'll be fine."

Vane's phone buzzed with a call. Without even looking at the caller I.D., she swiped it open to answer. "Vane."

Hannah's brow was furrowed in a frown-type of way that suggested she'd wanted to continue the conversation. Vane waved a hand at her and she rolled her eyes, but at least she left the office and closed the door behind her.

"Hey, baby," said a masculine voice that had her groaning. At least the rage that burned inside her every time she heard her ex's voice was enough to push the grief aside for the time being.

"Ross," Vane hissed. "Don't call me that. What do you want?"

"What makes you think I want something? Don't you trust me?" Ross said, his voice thick with a slimy unasked question. He was probably short on cash. That's usually why he called.

"We broke up, I'm not giving you any money, please stop calling before I file a protective order," Vane said as calmly as she could. It was not, in fact, very calm. Ross scoffed on the other end of the line.

"Vane, sweetheart, I miss you. I'm not calling with any like, interior motive."

"It's ulterior, you jackass." Vane's teeth ground together hard enough that her ears felt it. She breathed in through her flared nostrils and then out again as slowly as she could. She'd broken up with him more than a week ago, although, if she were honest, she'd been checked out of the relationship longer than that. "Forget my number, Ross."

"Look, Vane, I'm the best-"

She didn't hear him. She hung up and then blocked his number. Originally, she wasn't going to block him. It wasn't her style. Also, a life in the salon industry (and pretty much fending for herself everywhere else) had taught her sometimes it's better to stay in touch with your enemies so you could see what their next move was. But this was different. She wanted the cycle to be broken, and she couldn't do that if she kept accidentally answering his calls. She wanted to be free of his money requests, his backhanded compliments and... well. She couldn't deny her feelings for Hannah.

Wait, wasn't that a stage of this grief shit? Then yes, yes she could deny. Deny, deny, deny. With an angry huff, Vane straightened her mask and stood. She fucking had work to do. No time for anything else.

CHAPTER TWO

The rest of the day passed in a tense blur. Vane had never been particularly great at dealing with her emotions, which was probably something she should see a therapist about but it wasn't like doing hair came with health insurance. (It should. That one time she sliced her knuckle off would have been a lot better if she'd had insurance instead of an out of pocket ER visit.) Until she had insurance and a therapist, in that order, she was stuck in a cycle of "snap at everything that annoys me and, by the way, everything annoys me". Grief was tearing through her, leaving behind a feral monster who didn't really care much about anything. Everything was starting to feel overwhelming. Her break-up with Ross and now her grandma, knowing that she was all alone in this world that didn't care if it used you until you ran dry… feeling like she was going to be alone forever. It was all a little *much*. Bex, who was licensed in more stuff than Vane was but who specialized in nails, had holed up in the studio room she rented from Vane and only appeared to collect her clients. She'd rented from Vane for long enough to know when it was One of Those Days. At the end of her shift, Bex had twirled her keys and sent Hannah, who did not rent and was on commission, a sarcastically pitying glance.

"Adios, chicas," Bex had said, but what she really meant seemed to be, "Best of Luck, Hannah, hope you're still alive tomorrow."

She escaped through the back door before Vane could snap at her, slick, dark ponytail swinging as she went.

Bex's escape was better than Hannah's concerned looks. Hannah probably meant well enough, but her constant hovering only stoked the fire of Vane's misguided rage. Vane knew she should have canceled her clients and gone home, but home would only serve to remind her of all the things she'd lost to get where she was today. It was a journey she was proud of, but she wasn't sure it was worth it.

Fucking Ross. Fucking Gran. Fucking *everyone*.

Hannah made a quick exit during Vane's last color appointment of the day. Luckily, it was a client who had known her for a while. Not quite as long as Bernadette, but long enough that she called Vane's stormy moods an 'artist's temperament'. As soon as Hannah was gone, Vane admitted in hushed tones during the shampoo service what had happened, and her client was more sympathetic to her attitude. She did the blow-out and trim in near silence, and in the end, they were probably both more relaxed because of it.

After her client had gone, she took a few extra minutes to close up shop. She locked the back door, did the evening deposit, and managed to pack up her station and sweep without breaking into the ugly sobs that lurked in that cavernous, empty hole of a chest. Finally, with the key to her nasty old car in hand, she locked the front door and turned to look at the courtyard.

The first thing that had really charmed Vane about her salon was the location. It was just off of main street, set way back from the road in a strange courtyard, surrounded by other small businesses. It wasn't that cute at the time, because the hipsters hadn't discovered Quaint City, but it had so much potential. The buildings around the courtyard faced each other, with a little platform that came off of Gallery QC, creating a stage where they sometimes hosted live music. The courtyard, which Vane Attraction, Gallery QC and Devil's Stomping Grounds all shared, sort of forced the foot traffic to stop and gather around their businesses. It was a unique disruption of the other tourist trap shops that lined the main street. And Vane Attraction was right in the middle of it.

Eve, who owned Devil's, and Vane had pooled their resources over the summer and decorated the courtyard up since more people were sitting outside during the pandemic. They'd added twinkling lights and plants, more tables and chairs, and with autumn setting in, Eve had even set stacks of pumpkins and squash around. In the dim evening light, it was extremely sweet.

Vane didn't have much time to appreciate the pumpkins or feel proud at how she and Eve had changed up the area over the last decade because Hannah was waiting for her. She sat in one of the metal chairs outside of Devil's, with a paper to-go cup in her hand, shivering into her denim jacket. It was a bit cold, now that Vane was taking notice of the temperature. Hadn't it just been summer? Where had everything gone so quickly?

Hannah's curls twisted in the breeze. Her expression was tight and unreadable. Oh shit, was she about to quit? Vane couldn't blame her. Vane had been a fucking nightmare today. She grimaced as she watched Hannah stand.

Hannah wasn't as tall as Vane, and she was definitely rounder and more well-endowed, but what she lacked in height, she made up for in intimidation. Vane wondered a little about how bossy Hannah might be in bed versus how meek Hannah was in the salon, but she swallowed that thought right down. It wouldn't be good of her to get in the habit of imagining her employees in bed.

"Samantha," Hannah said. Annoyance flared, and so did Vane's nostrils at the sound of a name she absolutely detested. "I want to speak with you."

"You know," Vane attempted to make her voice into a casual drawl, but she wasn't convinced it was working. "It's such a pity that you struggle to remember my name."

"Your first name is Samantha," Hannah told her, and Vane merely angled her chin and arched her eyebrows.

"And I've repeatedly asked you to call me Vane, because no one calls me Samantha." The last person who had done so, and the only person Vane had tolerated it from, had apparently died two weeks ago and no one thought to inform her grandchild of the fact.

Hannah rolled her eyes. "Vane."

"Was that hard?" Vane purred sarcastically. She gestured for Hannah to sit down. Apparently, this was going to be a whole thing, and as defensive as Vane was feeling, she knew she had it coming to her. Hopefully the Devil's employees, who were usually in charge of coming out to stack the chairs and chain them against the building at the end of the day, wouldn't interrupt them. A glance through the window showed that the reason the chairs weren't already tucked away was due to some kind of event that looked suspiciously like an open mic night.

"I know you prefer your last name, but I've never been able to figure out why. It doesn't feel right," Hannah said. Her anxious fingers twisted together, but she sat across from Vane with that still sort of condescending look on her face. She pursed her lips. "You were an absolute monster today, I hope you realize."

Vane gave a casual shrug, "I can do what I want. I'm the boss."

Hannah's plush lips twisted into a frown. "No. You're not allowed to be like that. You're supposed to lead your team, not abuse it. You acted like-"

Hannah stopped herself. Her eyes went wide with shock and she clamped her lips together tightly. Vane latched onto that cut-off sentence like a snake on a live mouse.

"Go on," she dared Hannah through gritted teeth. "Say it."

"A diva," Hannah said smoothly as she tried to calm down. "You acted like a diva."

"That's not what you were going to say. You were going to say I acted like *him*," Vane snapped. She was wound too tightly to be having this conversation. "I am not as bad as Scott even on my worst day."

"Today *was* your worst day," Hannah shot back, her eyes firing with passion. "And you were exactly like Scott."

Hannah seemed to remember that Vane signed Hannah's paychecks, and her hands twisted together again in that anxious, worrying way she had. Vane wondered if Hannah was Catholic because it looked an awful lot like rosary bead twisting. "I'm merely saying that, while I understand the circumstances behind your attitude today, you cannot expect us to be happy about working in such an uncomfortable atmosphere. You were a beast."

"And are you speaking alone on this subject or have you and little Bexie-pooh had a bit of a convo behind my back?" Vane asked and she batted her eyelashes sarcastically. Hannah's expression was equal parts stormy and guilt-ridden.

"We care about you, *boss*," Hannah said slowly. Oh, shit, new kink unlocked. Vane almost blushed. "You seemed fine when I left you in the office. Did something else happen? Not that anything worse needs to have happened-"

"Not that it's any of your business what happened," Vane said, letting the word 'business' drawl out into a long line of hisses and z's. "But I broke up with Ross."

Hannah's eyes widened in shock. "You broke up with Ross?"

"Not today. I did it a week ago, actually. But he's been kind of stalking me since then and it's a pain. He called today and it just put me in a bad mood," Vane admitted. She felt distinctly uncomfortable. She hated this part. This part of being human, of having friends. Of having to admit that she was weak, somehow.

She'd been alone too long.

"So yeah, that plus finding out about my grandma on social, just. It was a lot today. I'm-" Vane choked on the word, but she said it anyway. "I'm overwhelmed."

Hannah's face melted into something soft and pitying. Of course Hannah, sweet and caring person that she was, thought Vane deserved pity. Vane was pathetic. "Oh, Ss- Vane."

Vane's throat started to close up at the correction in her name... and everything, if she were being truly honest with herself. The reality of what her aunt (and her parents, too, if she were being honest with herself) had done came crashing down around her. She tried to cover her sniffle with a sharp inhale. Hannah, wisely, stayed quiet.

She wasn't sure what Hannah's situation was, but she was fairly sure that Hannah understood about strained relationships with family. At the very least, when Hannah had quit working for Scott, there had been a slow transformation that suggested someone in her life who hadn't been supportive of her life choices was gone. She was still the only stylist in the world that Vane knew who actively chose to wear light colors in a salon setting, but the tent dresses and femme details that Scott tended to force upon his staff disappeared, replaced by a soft butch aesthetic that was driving Vane crazy the more she saw of it.

"Ross gets me all riled up. He's such a shithead," Vane said. Hannah's hand, so unlike her own in that it was soft and rounded where Vane's was too skinny and probably claw-like with her manicure, reached over the table to grip Vane's hand.

"He was a bit of a shithead," Hannah agreed with a sigh. Vane's eyes snapped to Hannah's face.

"You said a curse," Vane said, her lips twitching up. "You never curse."

"Well, Mr. 'Hey, I'm short on my rent because I went to Atlantic City with the boys and gambled my money away, can I have some of yours' probably warrants a curse. Or eight," Hannah said patiently. She squeezed Vane's hand. "Or, that time-"

"Yeah, no, I don't, um, need to relive all the times I took him back when I shouldn't have," Vane said. She huffed. "Don't date townies."

Hannah's hand drew back, but her lips curled into a secretive smile. "I don't know. They're not all bad, are they?"

"If they hang around with Ross then yes, yes, they are," Vane quipped. She toyed with a loose thread on the sleeve of her shirt. It was sticking out from under her signature leather jacket. Clothes in this industry never lasted long. Black was the standard uniform color, but between color and bleach stains and chemical processes, it was best not to get too attached to anything. Hannah was frowning again, but if she disagreed with Vane, she didn't say.

"I should get home. I know it's none of my business, but if you need the day tomorrow, we'll really be okay. You need to take care of yourself," Hannah told her. She was standing, and Vane could really get used to gazing up at Hannah like this. Vane licked her lips before she could stop herself.

"I'll be okay. See you tomorrow," Vane managed. Hannah smiled, but it was a sad one, and Vane hated every second of it. "Be safe."

"Always," Hannah promised. "You, too."

Vane watched as Hannah walked down the alley towards the parking lot tucked behind the main street. God, that rear end was particularly-

"Hey, girl," Eve called. Vane turned, her cheeks blushing a furious pink as she realized she'd been caught out staring at her employee's ass by another business owner. Eve tutted. "You look like shit."

"I feel like shit," Vane replied.

"That's bad marketing," Eve told her. It appeared whatever event had kept Devil's open later was over and Eve and her staff were beginning to tidy up for the night. Vane stood to allow Eve and Quita to start stacking courtyard chairs. Then, feeling entirely stupid, she started to help because of course she should, she was also a business that used the courtyard. Eve continued talking. "No one wants to go to a stylist who looks like shit."

"What do you care? You don't come over anyway," Vane teased. It was an old argument between them, one that had gone on since the salon had opened, and Vane used it any time she wanted to deflect from a topic. Eve snorted.

"How many times do I have to tell you to get a Black stylist and maybe I'll consider it? As it stands, Katrina knows just what to do with my hair when I walk in the door, no questions asked," Eve replied.

"What's Katrina getting paid?" Vane asked, thinking of the salon that she and Hannah had worked for. "Maybe I'll offer a higher commission."

"Oh, no, she went out and got herself one of those suites. She's doing so well, I'm proud of her. It's set up all cute when you walk in, and it's relaxing to know it's just you and your stylist. None of those grumpy salon managers stomping around all day, breathing down everyone's neck, trying to push product sales. It's peaceful," Eve told her. Vane nodded, knowing that her stupid mood had been tattled to the staff of Devil's. She tapped her lips with two fingers, a forgotten gesture that meant she was looking for a cigarette. Eve frowned. "I thought you quit."

"Oh, shit, I did, but it's been that kind of day," Vane told her honestly, huffing and then sucking in a lungful of air. She held it for a minute, wishing the oxygen would give her the hit she was looking for. "I found out Gran died. On fucking social media. The bastards didn't even have the courtesy to call me."

"Honey," Eve said quietly, but she knew Vane well enough to know she shouldn't hug. Vane wasn't a hugger on a good day. On a day like today? Well. Safer to just not.

"Yeah," Vane croaked, and she was definitely not sniffling. The noise that escaped her was just her clearing her throat. Through her nose.

"I'm here for you, if you need me," Eve said.

"I know you are. And, you know. Same. If you need anything," Vane replied.

"What could I possibly need? I've got a booming business, despite a global pandemic, and my beautiful partner is literally a therapist," Eve teased. Honey Sweet, Eve's partner, was a popular therapist in Q.C., and she saw a lot of the same queers that hung out in Eve's coffee shop.

"Well. Just in case you need back-up," Vane said.

"So, are you going to close?" Eve asked. "Or take a few days off?"

Vane frowned. "Why would I?"

"Girl, your nearest relation died, and they didn't even tell you. That's something that most people deal with in grief counseling."

"Normal people have steady paychecks and insurance. They don't live on commission, like a stylist." It was one of the downsides of the industry, really. Vane loved how creative and artistic she could feel while doing hair, but there were so many flaws with the system. Commission, insurance, injury, body aches, expensive supplies and classes- the list went on and on.

"We'll get you one of those crowd-funded things. I'm sure everyone would donate to letting you have some time off," Eve said.

"I wouldn't. Sorry, Vane, but I'm broke," Quita said as she stacked the final chair. Vane winked at her.

"I wouldn't want it anyway. I'll be fine," Vane replied. "Besides. If I leave those two alone for too long they'll burn down the salon. Bex was doing some viral thousand-coat-of-polish challenge today for her channel and the fumes were just disgusting."

"Ooh, I hope she posts the video soon. I love watching her stuff," Quita said. Bex had enough subscribers and sponsors that she could probably make streaming and content creation her entire career, but she loved doing people's nails and she had a loyal client base. Vane was lucky she was willing to rent the little studio room in the back of the salon.

"I'd love it if she learned to do that outside of working hours. You ever have to wrap a perm while she's doing some of that nail stuff? I thought I was going to gag earlier," Vane teased, but it was weak. She knew Bex's worth.

Eve was examining her nails. "You know, I do need a new nail girl."

Vane smiled. Say what you want about most small towns, but in the little courtyard pocket of Quaint City, they always found a way to support each other's businesses. "I'll talk to Bex and see if she's got an opening."

"You do that. And if you need anything," Eve said, letting the sentence trail off at the end. Vane nodded.

"I'll call."

They both knew her well enough to know she'd never call.

CHAPTER THREE

In theory, Vane knew she needed to do better. She refused to turn into a grumpy, tantruming mess like Scott had been. She wasn't setting a good example for her team by acting like a bitch. Tuesday had been in poor taste, but she could make Wednesday a better day. Tense and uncomfortable was not the vision she had for Vane Attraction. She could do better. She *would* do better.

Hannah was once again bouncing around the back door waiting for her. She was wearing her signature pale colors, even though it was October and most people switched to darker, muted tones, but she had a really unique khaki colored coat over her ensemble. It was one of those shirt-jackets, which was very butch of her, and looked vintage. It set off her long blonde curls and her bright eyes. She had a soft looking scarf wrapped around her neck and she was holding two paper cups from Devil's. Her hair floated like clouds in the early morning breeze.

Vane shivered. The heat had broken a long time ago in her poor little car, and the temperature had dropped dramatically compared to the previous day. Thanks, Maryland. Her black sweater was too thin to actually provide warmth, but she knew when she got dressed this morning that once she was under the heat of constant blow drying, she wouldn't be cold. After watching Hannah for longer than she intended to, and attempting to stifle the smile that wanted to stretch across her lips at the sight of her, she huffed and got out of her car.

And shivered again.

For all that global warming was real, Fall was definitely staking it's claim on Quaint City. The air outside was what most romance writers might call 'crisp', if this were one of Gran's old

AVERY MORSTAN

bodice rippers, but for Vane's thin frame that basically meant frigid. She shoved her bare hands in her pockets and tried to look sly as she slid up to Hannah.

"What's happening, hot stuff?" she said, and then instantly blushed as she realized she probably shouldn't have called Hannah hot. She sucked on her cheeks, feeling her lips twist into a pucker. Hannah was blushing, too. Vane truly felt like she'd be fine if the Earth opened up and swallowed her.

"Oh!" Hannah said. She sunk her teeth into the sweet pink lushness of her bottom lip, her eyes wide. "I, um. I was waiting for you. We- well, everything was so tense yesterday and I know that you have been under some stress from-"

She halted, and Vane had a feeling she had choked on the words, 'from finding out your grandma died'. Hannah's lips pressed together for a beat, and then she continued. "Just from everything. So I got you this. To make amends."

Hannah thrust one of the paper cups towards Vane, and then blushed and looked down, pulling the cup back in her direction. She tilted her head to the side to read the label and then held out the other cup instead. "Sorry! I got myself a mocha, which I probably shouldn't have because, you know. It's basically just a hot cocoa and those are so high in calories and-"

Vane took the offered cup, which the markings on the side identified to be black coffee, and cut her off. "Hey. I'm not Scott. You don't have to apologize for enjoying what you like, just because he had food issues."

Hannah blushed again, but she looked grateful. "Thank you. Sometimes it's just hard to forget the habit."

"I get it," Vane said with a nod. "I've been there. Sometimes I still feel bad when I actually accept a tip from a client."

Scott, the former employer they shared, had a habit of taking tips away from stylists for any little reason. He'd call it a 'tax on the electricity we used to train you' or 'education fund' or 'tip sharing for the assistants'. Once he'd had it, you'd never get your cash back. The first time Vane had managed to slip out of the salon with her actual tips in her actual pocket, she'd felt like

150

Charlie Bucket with a god damned Golden Ticket.

"I really am trying to forget," Hannah waved a hand. "Him. But it's hard."

"You'll get there," Vane told her. She was surprised at how gentle she managed to sound. She wasn't known for being super nice. "It takes time."

"Well, anyway, I thought since you look after all of us, maybe sometimes we should look after you. So I brought you a coffee. Also, Bex booked you a blow-out with a new client, and I overheard the call. You may need the caffeine. Or, I could take her. She sounds like a cantankerous old woman," Hannah said, and the adorable look on her face implied that cantankerous was supposed to be a curse word. Vane stifled a laugh.

"I can handle some nasty old woman," Vane promised her. "You work on your own clients."

If it were any other stylist, Vane would assume Hannah was just trying to be nice because old women might remind her of Gram, or something like that. But, in reality, Hannah's clientele were all pretty old. Like, she must have been the only stylist in beauty school that enjoyed rolling perms so now all the old women in town knew to go to Hannah if you wanted a fifties style blow out or an eighties perm wrapped. Hannah was really just being kind because she knew Vane liked youthful, instagram-worthy color services and trendy short cuts, and she didn't get a lot of that in a town like Quaint City.

"If you're sure," Hannah fretted, looking worried. Vane smiled and took a hopefully-suave-looking sip from her delicious coffee.

"Positive, hot stuff," she purred with a wink. Hannah blushed and they both went inside to start their day.

If there were a meme that could be inserted into Vane's life to show a hilarious turn of events, it would be someone in a bad French accent saying, "Two Hours Later". And Vane would know that only the millenials, like her, would appreciate the joke, but it would be worth it.

Two hours later, the most obnoxious, the most entitled antimasker sat down in her chair.

"Ma'am," Vane said, for what felt like the fiftieth time during the shampoo service. "I will not ask you again. Please pull up your mask."

"These stupid things don't actually work, you know," the old lady said as she glared up at Vane from inside the shampoo bowl. "The water is too hot. Make it colder."

Vane twisted the knob on the water to bring the temperature down. Meanwhile, the woman had her mask covering her mouth but not up over her nose. It was annoying the way a simple rule seemed so impossible to follow. The woman jerked, and some of the water sprayed down her sweater. "It's too cold now!"

"How about now?" Vane asked, her words slipping out from between gritted teeth. She twisted the knobs again.

"I'll have to deal with it, I guess," the woman said. Probably should've learned the woman's name. Vane was pretty sure it was Peggy. It was somewhere on the booking. Maybe-Peggy's eyes glared at Vane as she lathered soap over her damp hair. "You got any kids?"

What the *fuck*, Vane thought to herself. She tried to smile. She was a freaking professional, wasn't she? Vane could do this. "No, I don't."

"You better get on that. You're old. You'll be too late to have 'em," Maybe Peggy was saying. Vane switched on the water again to rinse the suds out of her hair. "Are you even married? Probably one of those lesbians. You've got too much eye stuff on, that's how I can tell. You'll die alone without kids to take care of you-"

Her words were cut off by an accidental spray to the face. Very accidental. Definitely a highly professional accident. Vane glanced up to where Hannah was standing at the counter, staring at Vane in horror as she realized... well, Vane couldn't assume it was horror at what Vane had done. The woman was horrible, Vane was being horrible- the entire situation was bad. So, safe to assume she had no idea what part of it Hannah had an issue with.

"Oh, I'm so sorry, ma'am, did I get you?" Vane said in a sugary sweet voice. The woman glared at her, but Vane managed to get her back to the styling chair. "Now, bear with me, ma'am, I don't hear so well over the dryer so I won't be as chatty while we're doing your style."

"Well, you better do it right. My granddaughter and I are going to lunch together and I want to look nice in case there's pictures," the woman said. Vane was willing to bet that this woman's granddaughter would not want photographic evidence of the two of them together, but then memories of her own Gran made her feel guilty. She'd give anything to see her grandmother again. The woman in her chair was scowling at her in the mirror, and she'd pulled her mask down low enough that her lips were visible when she spoke. "Are you sure you even know how to do hair?"

"Ma'am, I've been doing hair longer than you think," Vane managed. Her temper was twisting her stomach in knots. Maybe-Peggy regarded her with a skeptical stare.

"Mmhmm," she humphed dismissively. "Well, you better do it right. My little Tilly doesn't come to see me often." Vane started to tune her out, mindlessly working product through her thinning gray hair, until Maybe-Peggy got said, "And she's gotten into all this gay nonsense lately. We just keep hoping it's a phase she's going to grow out of."

Vane's teeth clicked together, but before she could throw the woman out of her chair, the front door to the salon opened.

The person who walked through was young. Vane couldn't even hazard a guess as to how old, but very young. They were wearing a pretty baggy tee shirt with an even baggier hoodie over it, but there was a small rainbow pin on the chest. Their hair was flipped over to one side. The woman in Vane's chair seemed to seethe.

"I told her mother to dress her appropriately," she hissed to Vane. But Vane's eyes were on the kid.

And then they were on Hannah.

Hannah, who was the most quiet, most polite girl in the

salon, went from hetero-passing to flamoyant gay man in a queer woman's body as if a fairy godmother had shown up and hit her with a disco-mirrored wand that sprayed glitter upon bodily contact. Her face transformed from that complacent sweetness that she was known for to an alien expression of excitement.

"Are you Tilly?" She screeched from halfway across the salon. The attention shifted. Suddenly, everyone in the salon was staring at Hannah instead of the child. The kid gave a swift nod. They looked almost embarrassed. Hannah snapped her fingers and hopped up and down.

"Yes! I saw you walking in, and you've got those throwback emo pants on, and I was like, this person is too cool, you have to be who I am waiting for. I used to have those pants when I was younger but mine were hot pink. I wore them with my flaming Vans," Hannah said, her voice booming through the salon. Vane stared at her in horror. Who the fuck was this? Hannah usually used the station next to Vane's chair, but there was an empty one closer to the door. They sometimes used the extra station when they had someone processing and they'd booked a cut in between, but Vane also had a vague hope of growing their team one day. Hannah's usual place was open, but she was guiding the kid to the further station, far away from the grandmother.

"I am so happy to see you. I bet we have so much in common," Hannah gushed as she snapped a cape around the kid's neck. "Now, your mom told me you wanted some color done before we trim and blow-dry."

The kid was still looking a little terrified, but they'd relaxed once they realized they weren't going to have to sit next to their grandmother. They also seemed utterly in awe of Hannah, but that was a feeling Vane was used to. Who wouldn't be in awe of Hannah's aggressive kindness?

Just before Vane switched on her blow-dryer to tune out Maybe-Peggy and finish the service, she saw Hannah bend down and very softly ask, "Pronouns?"

The kid's face was utterly transformed. Their eyes widened

as they realized they were safe in Hannah's chair. "They/them. And my name is Kai."

Hannah's face was a picture of understanding. "We're so very glad you came in today, Kai. Sit back and I'll get your color mixed up, okay?"

CHAPTER FOUR

The rest of the appointment went without a hitch. Once grandma had been released into the wild and all but escorted out of the salon by the kid's embarrassed mom, Vane had kicked back to watch Hannah work. Her skills were impeccable, of course, that's why Vane had hired her, but watching the way she comforted the kid and helped them feel at ease when nothing about their journey was going to be easy... well. Kai left with a pink shaved-sides wolf cut that matched their plaid bondage pants. Vane always said grow up into the adult you wish you'd had when you were a kid and Hannah was a shining example of that motto. The second the kid was paid and gone, Vane yanked Hannah through the salon and out the back into the alley.

"What the fuck was that, Hannah?" Vane asked, her lips definitely *not* twitching into a smirk. Yes, the transformation Hannah had undergone in just those few seconds when the child had walked through the door was breathtaking, to say the least. And, as someone who hadn't had the most accepting family, Vane could understand why Hannah had done it. Obviously. But she still wanted to hear those pretty lips explain themselves.

Hannah's cheeks tinted pink over her mask. "That grandmother was heinous."

Vane's smirk widened. "Yes. And?"

Hannah's eyes flashed angrily. She reached into her pocket for a hair tie and started trying to tame her wild curls. "Sometimes... well, you never know what a lack of support might do to a person. Children need encouragement, not some homophobic bullshit that makes them feel scared or too ashamed to express themselves."

Vane wondered if Hannah was talking from personal experience. She knew too well what it was like, what kinds of negative thoughts could whisper around, when you didn't feel loved. With a sigh, she put her hands on Hannah's shoulders and turned her so Hannah's back was to Vane. With her skilled, nimble fingers, she gently freed Hannah's mane from it's messy ponytail and started to smooth those white-blond curls into something more stylish. She could appreciate Hannah's casual (and by 'casual', Vane definitely meant 'non-existent') approach to hair and make-up, but they *were* in the beauty industry, for fuck's sake. Not to mention how it felt so good to be taking care of Hannah in return for Hannah taking care of someone else.

Vane was quiet for a moment while she worked, but eventually she spoke again. "Okay, I get it. But what if the old woman had custody and she does something nasty to your new friend once they get home?"

"But she didn't. I checked with the mom before I started the service," Hannah said. God, even her annoyed voice was precious. Patting her newly plaited hair gently, Hannah turned back to look at Vane with a fragile expression in her eyes and tension along her jaw that hinted at shyness. Something important was about to happen, wasn't it? "Could you... do you think you could cut my hair? After the shop closes for the day? I hate to ask, I mean, I shouldn't ask. You've had so much on your plate, but it's driving me crazy and-"

Vane reached out and gripped Hannah's hand. She squeezed it, hoping to cut this rambling off before it got too out of control. After the performance that Hannah had exhibited today on behalf of one small nonbinary child? Absofuckinglutely. "Sure. Just a trim?"

"More like a whole hack. It's- it's a lot, I know. And I get if you don't want to do it, but I was just thinking," Hannah used her free hand to fish out her phone from her back pocket, "something like this?"

It was a photo of a girl wearing a button-up shirt with extremely short cropped curls. Vane's eyes widened.

"Fuck, Hannah, that's a lot," Vane breathed. Hannah's hair, as it was, reached down past her shoulders and headed for her waist. This was a pixie cut. Vane looked over at Hannah. "Are you sure?"

Hannah's lips twisted from side to side as she considered. She took a deep breath and nodded. "I'm sure."

Vane thought about her clothes, and the subtle changes she'd been seeing in the stylist over the course of the last few months. "I know that Scott could be kind of homophobic himself. Did he keep you from getting the dyke haircut of your dreams?"

"You think this is a dyke haircut?" Hannah asked, and the rose shade in her cheeks turned into a deep crimson. She frowned. Then, she tilted her head up and scowled. "There's no such thing as a dyke haircut. It's just a haircut on a dyke."

Vane's eyebrows shot up to her hairline. She'd never expected to hear Hannah say it out loud. She grinned. "It's a cute haircut. I'd be happy to help."

She couldn't very well commend Hannah on doing what it took to make her client happy only to turn around and deny her in a moment when she needed the help the most.

"Oh! Really?" Hannah grinned, and Vane almost felt annoyed that she'd ever doubted that Vane would help her. "Thank you!"

Hannah got up on her tip-toes and pressed a kiss to Vane's cheek. Vane's lips parted. As quick and surprising as the gesture was, it did things to her. Surprising things. She had to choke on a gasp before Hannah pulled away to continue beaming at her like a little star. Vane managed to reign her face back into her trained grumpy scowl. "Of course. You're a stylist. You should have the hair that's going to help you feel most confident, not what some stuffy old boss thinks is ladylike."

Hannah grinned wider and nodded. "Excellent. I, ehm. I should get back inside. I've got a color client due any moment."

Vane was too charmed by Hannah, she thought as she watched the other woman walk back inside, bouncing as if her feet were made of clouds. This was entirely dangerous.

Vane had another couple of clients before she could get to

Hannah's cut, which was annoying because all she wanted was to get her fingers into Hannah's soft curls. Sadly, before Hannah, there was Tate.

Tate was one of those people you either loved or hated, but there was never any in-between. The crew of Devil's seemed to like them well enough, and Vane knew that they were friends with some of the locals, but they'd been fired from most of the surrounding businesses for their attitude. They had been coming to Vane for a long time for what they called the 'quintissential nonbinary cut', which meant long and curled on the top but shaved on the sides. They could be funny and almost sweet, or they could be sardonic and hard to handle. Vane liked their money, but she hadn't made up her mind about them as a person. She was pretty sure they were friends, or, would be, if Tate wasn't her client.

"Make it quick, eh? I got places to be," Tate said, arching an eyebrow as they slumped down into Vane's chair. They lifted a leg and propped one booted foot on Vane's station, which Vane kicked down immediately. She raised an eyebrow at them.

"Feeling frisky today?" she asked.

"Baby, I'm always frisky," Tate said. They were joking. They were always joking. That was probably why so many people didn't like them. If you were bad at reading people, you weren't going to see the laughter in Tate's eyes (or the way they used humor to keep everyone at arm's reach).

"Get fucked. Same as always?" Vane asked, motioning to the hair. Tate grinned up at her as she snapped a cape around their neck. Out of the corner of her eye, Vane could have sworn she saw Hannah looking... something. Off? What was with her?

"You know what I like," Tate flirted. Vane flicked on her clippers with a threatening glare. Tate winked. "Quita is threatening my life if I don't update my latest fanfic tonight. She really wants the new chapter. I told her that as soon as you were through with me, I'd go over to Devil's and get some writing time in."

That... was a lie. Interesting, Vane thought.

"Well, I'll probably see you there after I close up shop," Vane said. As she spoke, again, she caught Hannah freezing up as she tidied around the shampoo station. Did Hannah have a problem with Tate? She had nonbinary clients herself, so it couldn't possibly be that Tate used they/them pronouns, right?

"Careful. I think Jesse had another audition this weekend. I've got a bad feeling," Tate said quietly. "I know it's been rough for them. There might be drama if he stops by."

"Jesse doesn't scare me," Vane teased. She carefully trimmed at the overgrown sides of Tate's head, stopping just before the back. "Want me to leave it a mullet? You'd look fantastic with a mullet."

"As much as I always want to look gayer, I think we both know why that's a bad idea," Tate said, tilting their chin up as they eyed themselves in the mirror.

"Halloween is coming up," Vane pointed out, but she continued trimming the back of Tate's head. "The eighties vampire look would suit you."

Tate snorted. "I don't doubt it."

Vane wasn't sure what everyone else knew, but she'd had Tate in her chair for enough years that she knew their parents were bigoted assholes. Sadly, Tate's inability to keep their foot out of their mouth resulted in changing jobs just enough times that they could never seem to get a security deposit together in order to leave their house. Part of her job as a stylist seemed to be keeping everyone's secrets, so she never said anything to their mutual friends, but sometimes she wished she could start a crowdfunding thing to get Tate a new home. She put down the clippers after edging Tate's neck a little, and then picked up the spray bottle. She spritzed down the top of their head and started to trim. As she lifted the hair, she happened to glance over at Hannah. Hannah's cheeks were bright pink over her mask, and she was definitely polishing the same bottle of shampoo that she'd been polishing five minutes ago. Vane pursed her lips.

Tate was watching Vane watching Hannah.

"Speaking as an author of romantic fanfic," Tate said in a

voice that made Vane want to stab them in the throat.

"Bad fanfic. And an Ace author, anyway," Vane said with a frown.

"Hey! Ace does not by default mean sex repulsed. I know stuff about romance and all the shit that comes with it," Tate said defensively. It made Vane wonder if that was actually true. "She's jealous."

Vane's eyes snapped back to Hannah. there was no way she could possibly be jealous. Hannah wasn't looking at them, but her posture did seem a little... off.

"You're crazy," Vane muttered. She turned back to Tate and started trimming the longer top pieces. It wasn't that she wasn't confident, she was confident. She knew that she was pretty attractive, no qualifiers needed. She took care of herself. Not in that kind of bullshit Instagram fitness influencer way. As she edged out of her thirties, there was a softness to her body that she wasn't used to, but she'd always been taller than most other girls and she was a cosmetologist so she needed to have her hair done, her nails perfect and her make-up on. She looked good. And she knew it.

Did Hannah think she looked good? The idea made her shiver.

"She's cute, Vane. Don't wait too long," Tate said, giving her a lascivious wink.

"Get bent, Tate," Vane replied.

"I have a date later. I just might," Tate chuckled, knowing full well that they had no intention of getting bent or fucked any time soon. They winked again and headed out. Hannah had been sweeping up around Vane's station while she checked Tate out, and now she hovered nervously near the chair waiting for her own turn.

"Are you sure? If you're too tired," Hannah started but Vane waved her off.

"Get a cape," she said. She thought better of her tone for a second and tried to gentle it with an added, "And you don't have to sweep for me. I'm not Scott. I can handle myself without an assistant."

"But it might be nice to have someone help you anyway," Hannah replied pointedly. Well. It didn't hurt, that's for sure.

"Speaking of nice," Vane teased. She'd picked up her favorite shears and was rocking them back and forth along a leather cleaning cloth. Hannah's eyes were definitely tracking the movement of her hand. "Go get cozy in the bowl. I'll wash you out first."

"Oh, that's so much effort. You could just spray it down," Hannah said. The way her adorable eyes widened at the idea of someone shampooing her hair was just precious. Vane grinned.

"We're helping each other. Now, let's get you all wet," Vane said, leading her in the direction of the shampoo area. The small gasp that Hannah made at the joke- part affronted, part something else entirely- was worth it. Hannah leaned back in the shampoo chair and Vane started to warm up the water, gently swishing the nozzle back and forth.

"Just the sound of that is nice," Hannah breathed. Vane smiled.

"One of the other places I worked at, before I worked with Scott, showed me this technique. It's a little hypnotizing, listening to the sound of the water near one ear and then the other," Vane said softly. 'The Shampoo Experience', as the salons always called it, was supposed to be your time to relax your clients and get them all warmed up to hand over their wallets for services. Or, that's how it always seemed for Vane. In reality, she also enjoyed giving her clients a few minutes to chill and forget their troubles while she washed their hair.

"Ohh," Hannah breathed in a way that made Vane squirm as the water hit her scalp. "That's perfect. How did you know?"

I know you, Vane wanted to say, but instead her mouth supplied, "I'm a professional. It's my job to know."

She wanted to make this good for Hannah. She wanted to take care of someone, for God's sake, the way she should've- hmmm, best save that thought for a future therapist, honestly. She could focus on this, on now, and how after staring at

Hannah's ass for a whole summer she was going to have those luscious locks in her chair.

"Well, you're very, very good," Hannah said in a low voice that shot straight to Vane's libido. She flushed under her mask and started to lather up Hannah's hair. "Oh! Oh, my God!"

Vane's lips twitched to the side in a cocky smile. Hannah's eyes stayed closed but it looked like she was making a considerable effort. "Good?"

Vane was entirely proud of her massage technique. It had taken a while, but the way she used her thumbs to go down the center of the head, then back along the parietal ridge and up the sides, was something not many other people would think to do. She wasn't scrubbing, like Hannah was a puppy at the groomers, she was working the product through with all her fingers and a firm, constant pressure.

"Christ," Hannah breathed and Vane's heart soared at the blasphemy. "You are amazing at that."

"I'm glad you're enjoying it," Vane said. Hannah was enjoying it, and she enjoyed the conditioner, too. Once all the purple-tinted product was washed away, she wrapped a towel around Hannah's hair and helped her to stand.

"I don't know if I can feel my feet again after that," Hannah teased. She did look a bit shaky, but she was up and walking towards Vane's chair.

"I used some of the purple conditioner to bring out your natural tones," Vane said as she gently squeezed the towel over Hannah's hair so as not to rough up the cuticle. Once Hannah was settled, she pulled her mask up over her eyes, exposing those beautifully full lips. Things Vane would have to not think about when she was on her own time: 1. Hannah blindfolded.

"What are you doing?" Hannah asked.

"Well, I'm wearing a mask and we've been in close contact so I'm pretty sure I'm not at risk. I want this to be a surprise for you," Vane told her. The way Hannah's breath quickened made Vane swallow. "Now, be a good girl and sit still for me."

"Whatever you say, boss," Hannah replied, her voice rough

and low. Vane had to bite her lip to get her brain to work again.

The cut went smoothly. Of course it did, Vane was incredibly skilled. She was proud of the abilities she'd honed in her decades in the industry. And while she cut, Hannah talked.

"My family isn't so awful, actually. They think styling hair is beneath me. My mom constantly complains about how well I did in school and I should be something more substantial like a teacher or a writer, but I like doing hair," Hannah said. Vane lifted section after section, cutting heavy curls and shaping what was left. "I got bullied a lot in school, though, and I just felt there was a gap in the industry for queer voices. We deserve safe places and technicians who can help us feel safe."

"I was wondering if you were giving yourself a dyke makeover for a reason," Vane said as she started to work on the top section of Hannah's hair. The urge to take her time and keep Hannah in her chair as long as possible, so it was just the two of them in this calm little bubble, was overwhelming. "You were wearing dresses and then it's corduroy trousers and button-ups. You got very dapper almost overnight."

"I've just decided that without Scott's heteronormative dress code I was finally free to express myself," Hannah said. She sighed. "My mother hates it, but luckily I don't have to see her every day."

"Well, you look good in a bowtie, sugar," Vane said. It had been one day in July when Hannah had come in wearing an honest-to-God bowtie and vest. Vane had almost choked.

"Thank you," Hannah said softly. Vane snipped a few more strands in silence before reaching for the pomade she liked to use for soft masculine styles.

"Are you ready to remove your blindfold?" Vane asked. Hannah's cheeks dusted again, but when she answered, Vane was not ready.

"I don't know. I rather like being blindfolded by you," Hannah said. Vane couldn't trust herself to respond. She simply reached around and slid the blindfold down.

Hannah's face was exuberant. She was stunned, she was in

awe, she was delighted- She was everything Vane had hoped for. Her curls, which were more defined now that there wasn't so much weight pulling down on the hair, framed her face like an angel's halo. It was a white, curling cloud of perfection.

"Oh Vane," Hannah said. "It's perfect."

No, that would be you, Vane wanted to say. She shrugged, lifted her lips in a cheeky smile and said, "I know."

CHAPTER FIVE

Vane had only just sat down at one of the tables at Devil's with a decaf latte in hand when Jesse arrived, fresh from rejection.

"I give up!" Jesse said loudly as he flopped down into a chair at Devil's. Jesse was Quita's boyfriend and an actor in the local community theater scene. Sadly, the small town of Quaint City just wasn't ready for a trans leading man.

Both Quita and Vane were fresh off a long shift of being on their feet for hours on end with not enough breaks and were not likely to be the sympathetic audience Jesse was hoping for. Quita barely managed to look up from her phone, with her brows knitting together.

"Didn't get in?" she asked.

"Yup," Jesse said, making sure to pop the 'p' sarcastically. Vane raised an eyebrow and waited for an explanation. Jesse sighed. "This director was mentoring me through the pandemic, really coaching me, and she said she wanted to do better about creating space for trans folks in theater. I thought that meant she was encouraging me to audition for her, but the cast list just came out and everyone is cis and, if I know the other actors like I do, straight."

"That's frustrating," Quita said. She reached out to grip Jesse's hand and gave it a loving squeeze, but her voice held a monotone quality that said, 'been there, done that, the cast is probably all white, too'. In fact...

"It gets worse. They're all-" Jesse held up their free palm and tapped it, grimacing as they did. Quita rolled her eyes.

"Honey, I could've told you they were going to be all white," she said. "It's one of the reasons I stopped going to auditions for you. This place is too small for people that look like us."

"Yeah, I know. But I'd hoped," Jesse groaned. It was a raspy, rumbling sound. Vane was pretty sure Quita had said Jesse started on hormone treatment, but even if he hadn't, he was making an effort to change his voice. "I really wanted to be Mr. Darcy, too. That's such a classic role."

"You know perfectly damn good and well that they weren't going to cast you as a lead, *if* they cast you at all," Quita said in a tone dripping with disappointment, as if Jesse had done something particularly stupid. "And, at least you tried. You showed up for your community. We just need to find you a more accepting community."

"Why not here?" Vane asked, raising her eyebrows. If their wide, deer-in-headlight stare was any indication, they had both forgotten about her. She gestured around them at Devil's, at the cozy atmosphere, and shrugged. "Look, it's a pretty large space. Do some kind of immersive theater event and advertise it by releasing snippets on the clock app. Right? I bet Tate could help. They write, don't they? Y'all just did that poetry whatever the other night and Eve said she wanted more events to happen. Do a themed show and cast your friends. Force the community to see you as a legitimate performer."

"Holy fuck," Jesse breathed, full of awe.

Quita was less impressed. "Hold up-"

"Quita!" Jesse said excitedly, squeezing her hand and shaking it. "Tate writes for the detective-what's his name? The Loxley somethings. That's recognizable and still in the public domain! It's better than Mr. Darcy! Is Tate here? I gotta tell them. Eve's definitely going to love this - Tate! Be back in a sec, y'all."

Vane was no casting expert, but she was pretty sure that Jesse was not a 'Mr. Darcy' type. Jesse had 'Bingley Golden Retriever Boyfriend' written all over him. He bounced to his feet and went in search of Tate, who was holed up in a far corner table with their laptop in front of them. Vane was smiling until she caught Quita's eye.

"What?"

"I'm just worried about him, is all," Quita said softly. "He's been rejected so many times. I mean, I love him, but what if he's just a bad actor? Or what if we get hate crimed for putting on some gay play? Or what if Eve says no?"

"Do you think Eve is going to say no?" Vane asked, taking a sip from her latte. Quita scowled.

"No. I think she's going to eat this shit up," she admitted. "She's been weird lately, though. Like, I don't want him to get all excited and then it falls through."

"What do you mean, 'Eve's been weird'?" Vane asked.

"She keeps getting on me to find my purpose or something. I've been really happy being her, I mean, manager only I'm not her manager? She's been weird. I think the shop might be in trouble," Quita said, whispering the last part. Vane frowned. She was pretty sure the shop wasn't in trouble. Or, it shouldn't be. It was the only place in QC to get coffee that didn't have a Mc in front of the name, and it was constantly packed.

"Look, if she says no, I'll let them do it in the courtyard. They can even use the salon as a dressing room," Vane told her. "We'll make it work, okay? I'm just tired of people putting other people down this week. I had to do something."

Quita arched an eyebrow. "His pronouns are he slash him."

"And I see him dragging Tate into this, creating a collective 'them'," Vane argued. "I see Jesse for who he is. Trust me."

"My mom always said you can't trust anyone that isn't family," Quita replied. It was Vane's turn to arch an eyebrow.

"Yeah, and look how that's working out for me."

Quita smiled. "You trust Hannah well enough."

"I don't have a choice. She's one of the best stylists in town. If it weren't for the stupid non-compete, she could work anywhere," Vane said.

"Non-compete?"

"Pretty standard in the industry, and they don't usually hold up in court, but basically her old boss made her sign a contract saying she wouldn't work within a certain distance around his salon. I had one. My salon is six inches over the end of the line and I know it pisses him off," Vane said with a devious snicker.

"Actually, I never signed mine," Hannah's voice said from over Vane's shoulder. Vane twisted in her seat to look back at Hannah, who was radiating an aura of smugness. She shrugged. "It's one of the things that caused our falling-out. He wanted the non-compete, and I told him it was nonsense and I wasn't doing it."

"Good for you, girl. That's fucked up," Quita said.

"Why are you here?" Vane asked, but she was interrupted by a commotion from the corner where Jesse had been badgering Tate. Tate had pushed their chair back loudly and stood, closing their laptop with a firm snap that probably wasn't good for it. Jesse's face was pleading, but Tate's was a storm of emotion.

"But Tate!"

"Not after what you did with Erin!" Tate snapped.

"Denver didn't care!"

"It's the principle of the thing!"

Jesse's face flicked from Tate to Quita and back again, his eyes incredibly hurt. "But she was just a fling! And I apologized! Quita said we're cool!"

Tate, who was halfway out of the shop, turned and glared before biting out, "Not. On. Your. Life."

Jesse didn't have the sense God gave a bedbug. He gestured to the rest of the cafe, who were all staring at the two of them. "Look! It's like a floor show! They love it. Let's give the people what they love."

"I'm going to murder you," Tate said, and they stormed out of the coffee shop with Jesse tight on their heels.

"I mean, if that's the plot you're after, but I think murdering me would fall under the 'bury your gays' thing and the audience would hate it," Jesse was saying. Hannah, Vane and Quita watched them both leave before Hannah slid down into the seat next to Vane. She shrugged.

"Forgot something at the salon. And you said you'd be here," she said, answering the question in Vane's eyes like a psychic.

Vane had been wondering why Hannah was back after such a long day. Vane turned to Quita.

"Think Jesse'll talk them into it?"

"Possibly," she said, already staring down at the phone in her hand. Vane frowned.

"You know, being a stylist is almost as good as being a therapist. If you wanted to talk about it, I could-"

"It was nothing. We're open, there's going to be others. I'm just disappointed that's who they picked first," Quita grumbled. "I'm dating someone else, too. Just not a bitch who fucked over one of my friends. But baby needed to learn a few things and I couldn't teach him that." Vane would have to fill Hannah in later on how Denver's ex, Erin, had been a giant transphobic bitch up until she decided it was okay to screw around with Jesse. That seemed like a 'later' kind of talk, though.

"Okay," Vane said, twisting her lips to the side. The firm tone suggested that Quita did not want to talk about it further, which was fine but also had Vane a little worried. She sighed. "You want to date me?"

"Not on your fucking life," Quita said. She looked up from her phone without actually looking up. "You're a mess."

"True. I'm hot, though," Vane said with a wink. She was really just teasing, because Quita seemed to need it, so she laid on a thick wink. Quita laughed and returned to her phone.

"Believe you me, I know where your heart is, even if you don't," Quita said with a not-so-subtle glance at Hannah. Vane blushed.

"You want to get out of here?" Vane asked, deciding to ignore Quita for her own good. "I don't want to go home yet and I could use something stronger than coffee."

"Sure. Sounds good to me," Hannah said. She smiled at Quita. "You want to come with?"

"Nah, you kids go ahead. I've got things to do," she replied.

Vane rolled her eyes. She stood, and then offered her hand to Hannah, who looked delighted to take it. "Night, Quita. Don't work too hard."

CHAPTER SIX

Hannah in the streetlights of Quaint City was the closest Vane was ever going to get to seeing an angel. With autumn creeping in, it was getting darker earlier, and fairy lights had been strung up in the trees that lined Main Street as a way of prepping for Christmas. Quaint City was big on Christmas celebrations. Hannah's stark white curls shining in the shadowy light cast by the fairy lights was just a beacon that Vane didn't know she needed.

Vane smiled at Hannah. "I'm not ready to go home yet, are you?"

Hannah's answering smile was as bright and warm as the fairy lights. "No. Definitely not."

"I know of a little place up the street," Vane said, sucking on her teeth just a little. She nodded in the direction of the bar that she was thinking of. "You want to go see if they're open?"

Hannah hesitated. "I am supposed to do the opening shift tomorrow. I wouldn't want my boss to be upset with me."

"I'll put in a good word for you," Vane said with a wink she hoped had half of Tate's charisma. She did feel a little smarmy saying that, but the look on Hannah's face made it all worthwhile. Hannah had wanted to say yes, but Hannah wanted to make sure Vane was okay with it. And Vane was more than okay. She added, "We don't have to get completely blitzed or anything. I just want a drink, maybe some darts or pool, and a little bit of conversation with someone I'm fond of." Vane shrugged. "Could be fun."

"I'm fond of you, too," Hannah said, and she reached out to take Vane's arm. She squeezed. "I'm… out of practice. It's been a long time since I've gone to a bar with a friend."

"Same, honestly," Vane told her. "You don't have to. I just thought it sounded kind of fun and I really didn't want to go home."

"I promise, I want to. Let's go," Hannah assured her. They started to walk, arms brushing, along the streets of Quaint City.

"You know, you've worked for me for a while. I don't think I know anything about you," Vane said. She swallowed hard. "You know about.. about how my grandma meant so much to me, and how she raised me and all."

"I don't know why," Hannah pointed out. "Why did she have custody of you? Of course you don't have to say, that's probably a rude question-"

"No, no, it's fine. My parents kicked me out when they found out I was queer. Gran took me in, encouraged me," Vane huffed out a heavy breath rather than start to cry, which she was so close to. "And then I abandoned her."

"You didn't abandon her," Hannah said. "Everyone deals with grief differently."

"I should've gone over more. I just couldn't stand to see her suffer like that," Vane said. She shrugged. "It was selfish."

"I'm sure she knew that you loved her," Hannah said quietly. They were almost to the bar, and they didn't speak again until they entered and were ordering their drinks. Hannah twirled on the barstool like a kid, sipping her hard cider.

"My mother was fairly supportive, actually," Hannah said eventually. "My father seems uncomfortable, but it was never hard for me at home. They still tried. I feel incredibly lucky. But I also feel sort of... like maybe I should have suffered."

"No, no," Vane told her. "No one should have to suffer."

"I loved this girl once, and she had been in a situation similar to yours and I just found it so hard to relate to her. It was a long time ago, I was very young, but I didn't allow for some of the mental processing that comes with that sort of trauma. I was a dick. I feel pretty sick when I look back on how I treated her," Hannah admitted softly. She turned on her stool again, seemingly to distract herself. "And then when I got the job at Scott's salon, he was really adamant about protecting his image from the start, so I just sort of went quietly back into the closet. Wore dresses, kept my long hair, but I felt miserable. I felt like I was hiding. It's nothing compared to what my ex went through but I feel like I have a better understanding of what happened to her now. I should apologize one of these days."

"Are you still in contact with her?" Vane asked, feeling an alien surge of jealousy at the idea of some other woman, but trying to tamp it down as well. She knew that jealousy was normal, it was how you reacted to it that made you an asshole.

"Not really. Sometimes we send each other memes, but it was a long time ago," Hannah said. She took another sip of cider. "We're different people than we used to be, and mores the better for us."

"Well, aren't we a barrel of fun," Vane said, trying to lighten the mood. She looked around. "Okay, so there's no darts but they do have some ancient ass skeeball machines back there. Wanna give it a go?"

"That sounds fun," Hannah said, and she slipped off her stool. They wound their way through the crowded bar to the back corner where there were old arcade games, like pinball and skeeball. Vane slid a few singles into the quarter machine, feeling a bit like she was doing laundry, and took out the coins. She handed some over to Hannah.

"You want to bet on anything?" Vane asked. Hannah grinned.

"I bet I can beat your score by a hundred. I used to be an excellent bowler," Hannah told her. God save Vane from soft little butches who talked like nursery school teachers, because damn Hannah was cute.

"You got it, but I warn you, I sure play a mean skeeball," Vane teased, singing the last part of the sentence. Hannah winked.

"I'm not worried," she said.

"So what are the stakes? I mean, we're going to need to play for something," Vane said as Hannah was pushing dollar bills into a coin change machine. The quarters made a musical crashing as they dispensed.

"Hmm, you've already cut my hair," Hannah said thoughtfully. "So I'm not really sure what you have to offer me."

"I can make a pretty good omelet," Vane said with a shrug. Hannah's eyes were an array of emotions. There was something deep and hungry, and bright and inquisitive at the same time. She tipped her cider to her lips, but just before taking a sip, her tongue darted out to dab suggestively at the corner of her mouth. Vane almost choked.

"Omelets are my favorite," Hannah said softly.

"Well, what do I get? If I win?" Vane asked. Hannah put her drink down and inserted a quarter into the machine. The smooth wooden balls made a satisfying sound as they rolled into place. Hannah picked one up and shifted it from one hand to the other, and she angled her head confidently.

"You won't," she said. She turned and threw the ball. Vane watched Hannah's backside more than she did Hannah's actual throw, but when the ball sank into the hundred point hole, she had no doubt that Hannah was correct.

Hannah looked over her shoulder and smirked. "Your turn."

CHAPTER SEVEN

Vane was utterly creamed.

Oh, and she lost.

Hannah might have been an angel in the shop, but she was a demon when it came to skeeball. And Vane loved every minute of it. Especially when, after their final round, Hannah had pulled Vane in for a hug that went on… long enough for them to get kicked out of the bar. And then there was a kiss in the alley. And another. And another. Each hazy, cider-coated memory led to a new discovery until Hannah's hands were smoothing down over Vane's tight jeans while Vane unlocked her apartment.

Vane had always operated under the assumption that, while she was thin and what she had was tight for its age, she did not actually possess an ass, but there was sweet little Hannah proving her front by cupping what was there very appreciatively. Vane smiled.

"Someone's excited," Vane teased as she pushed the door to her apartment open. She led the way for Hannah, closing the door behind them. Vane's apartment was a lot like the salon. It had that mixture of gaudy and goth that the salon office had. It said, "It wasn't just a phase and I may have spent too much time in thrift stores as a youth". Hannah smiled.

"It's very you," Hannah said. Vane wrapped Hannah up in her arms and kissed her. This time, it was sweeter than the other bar kisses had been. It wasn't hurried and there was no one here to give them a hard time. Hannah's lips were full and addictive.

"Wait 'til you see the bedroom," Vane said. She bit her lip and raised her eyebrows. She wanted this. She'd wanted Hannah for a long time, but now she was worried. "Are you sure this is okay?"

"I have wanted to see what your hands could do since the first time I saw you pick up a pair of shears," Hannah said, licking her lips. "Show me your room."

Vane smiled and kissed her again. Her hands gripped Hannah, unwilling to let her go, one just under her bra band and one settled in the small of her back. She smiled and then pinched at the back clasp. Hannah gasped, and giggled.

"Cheeky!" she said, but she followed when Vane sauntered back towards the bedroom.

"I like my guests to be comfortable," Vane argued. She flicked on the lamp next to her bed. Maybe one day she'd grow out of her goth phase, but that day was not today. The walls were painted a deep, deep burgundy, which was one of her favorite colors. She'd actually had her hair that color for years until the cherry cola style of the nineties gave way to the stripper stripes of the early oughts. The lamp was a thrift store find that was a nude woman's torso, and she'd painted it gold and stuck a black lampshade on it. You didn't grow up poor without learning how to make old stuff look good. She tugged Hannah down onto her dark sheets.

"This is very comfortable," Hannah agreed, looking down on Vane with those bright eyes that Vane adored. She ran her hands over Vane's arms, not quite pinning, but also firmly enough that she was suggesting Vane stay still. "You are gorgeous."

"Nnuh, you," Vane managed eloquently. Hannah's lips twisted upwards in a little smirk before she leaned down to press her lips to Vane's again.

"Tell me what you like," she whispered in Vane's ear. Then, she pressed her hot lips against the skin just underneath, trailing down Vane's throat. She worked her way back up, licking along Vane's skin. "I want to know what you want."

'You' would have been too easy an answer, but it was an honest one, at least. Vane gasped as Hannah nibbled gently on her throat. "Well, we could finish taking your shirt and bra off as a start."

Hannah pulled back. Smiling down at Vane, and looking

rather coy, she slipped her buttons open one by one. Each flick of her finger was meant to drive Vane mad, and Vane loved every moment of it. Hannah straddling her, Hannah taking her clothes off, all of it. Vane pressed up with her thigh, giving Hannah some pressure to grind onto as her bra followed her shirt. A gorgeous flush was starting to spread across Hannah's collar bone.

"God, I've thought about this so often," Vane said. She cupped the full weight of Hannah's breasts, giving them a gentle knead. "This okay?"

"Okay? Please. I've thought about bending you over the wash station more than once. This is incredible," Hannah said. "Yeah, gosh, that feels amazing."

"Gosh?" Vane snickered. But before Hannah could protest, Vane was pushing up to latch her lips around the rosy bud of Hannah's left nipple. She teased along the outside of that precious little nub before taking it again into her mouth. Hannah was left gasping.

"Vane," Hannah said. "You're too- you have- the clothes! Vane, please, I need to see you."

"You, too," Vane insisted, although she was aware that she was wearing more than Hannah was at this point. Vane let Hannah slide her own shirt up and over her head, flinging it to the floor, before both of their pants joined them in a puddle. Splayed out naked on her bed under Hannah was an experience Vane was never going to forget. Vane wanted to touch everything. She wanted to feel everything about Hannah, the press of their bodies together, her fingers digging into soft hips.

"V-Vane," Hannah said. For all that she started on top, she was starting to tremble apart. Vane grinned.

"On your side?" Vane managed. Hannah nodded and soon they were wrapped up in each other's arms again. Their mouths worked together while their fingers explored, breaking apart to tell each other 'yes' or 'not there' or 'slightly to the left'. Soon, it was all Vane could do to concentrate on moving her own hands while she watched the breathtaking expressions that crossed Hannah's features. How Hannah wanted to watch Vane, too, but she had trouble keeping her eyes open. How Hannah liked Vane's middle and ring fingers curved just so, while Vane's other hand helped by keeping a rhythmic pressure on her clit. How when Hannah finally clenched around Vane, she gasped like a romance novel heroine. It wasn't too much longer, or maybe it was and Vane was just enjoying herself so much she didn't keep track, before Hannah had worked out the spot that would have Vane crying out her name.

They cuddled for a while, blissed out with sweat coating their bodies. Vane snickered. "At least we're not guys. Nothing is unpleasantly sticky."

"True. Should probably still use the restroom, though," Hannah pointed out, but she'd started to snore softly where her head was cuddled up on Vane's shoulder. Vane was too boneless to move, and Hannah's weight was comforting against her. Eh. They'd work it out eventually, right? Vane tugged the comforter up over them both, snuggled in, and fell fast asleep.

Vane woke up in her apartment alone. For a second, she wondered if she'd dreamt it all, but the scent of Hannah, sex and that pomade Vane had worked through those soft curls the day before all lingered on Vane's bedsheets. All of it seemed too good to be happening to her. This didn't feel one-night-stand-ish. After all, she was Samantha "every boyfriend I've ever had needed therapy" or "every girlfriend I've ever had was just experimenting" Vane. This felt real. Like a real girlfriend that Vane could *really* bring hot cocoa to when she went to the shop this morning.

The second thought she had, after wondering if it all had been a dream, was that it was typical. Of course she woke up alone. She was someone that everyone always wanted to fuck but no one ever wanted to make eggs with. Except...

Except that wasn't fair to Hannah.

Hannah was unlike anyone that Vane had ever met. Hannah

179

was a golden thing, a blessing and a promise. She had taken that nonbinary child under her wing and protected them from their family for a few hours. She was the same Hannah who aired out the salon so Bex didn't fume her brains out doing a crazy video or who swept up after Vane so no one tripped on slippery hair. She was a lot of things, and she certainly had flaws, but Hannah was not a shitty person.

"I have to open tomorrow," Hannah had said last night.

A glance at the alarm clock on the nightstand (Vane was old, give her a break) said that it was ten in the morning. Hannah was at work. Because if one thing could be said about Hannah, it was that she was responsible to a fault.

Vane collapsed against her pillows with a stupid smile spreading over her face. She wriggled in the fabric, feeling it slide over her naked body. Hannah was at work. She'd be able to see her in just a few short hours.

Or, she could go see her now. She was the boss, after all.

Vane leaned over to her nightstand to check her phone. She opened the message from Hannah first.

You're sleeping like the dead, but I kissed your forehead before I left. See you at work.

Such a proper little lady, using correct grammar and punctuation and everything. Vane smiled so hard her cheeks ached.

Then from Bex.

Your girlfriend is whistling. You two finally shack up? She looks entirely too happy and won't say anything.

Fucking hell, Bex probably had some kind of bet going or something as to when it was going to happen. Before Vane could even text back, she received another one from Bex that said, "Tate won. Fuck this."

Vane snorted. Well, that's what Bex got for gambling.

She put her phone back down and closed her eyes. She was going to be sad for a long time. Her grandma was gone and she'd never even gotten the proper chance to say goodbye. That was something only time could heal. But there were things to look forward to, too, and they were important things. They were things to hold on to. There was Hannah, and all of the potential there, and there was the salon, which was doing well. There were hot ciders from Devil's Stomping Grounds and maybe she could con the team into going apple picking for publicity photos, but also because it seemed like a really cute thing to do with the beautiful people she worked with. Especially Hannah.

Vane lay staring at her ceiling for a long time. She knew she had to get a move on if she wanted to treat Hannah to that coffee. She desperately needed a shower and she wanted to look particularly sexy for her little soft butch. But there was something still nagging at her.

Don't start drama, she thought to herself. But then decided that she hadn't started the drama, but she could finish it. Her parents, and by proxy her aunt, had started all the drama when they decided to let their religious beliefs overshadow their love for their child. They started all of this when Vane became more of a thing, more of a social status, to them, than an actual person with real feelings. She deserved her family's support and, in the end, she'd only had Gran.

She flicked open her phone, smiling at the idea that she could send Hannah 'good morning, gorgeous' texts. So she did. Then, she opened the app that had started this all.

Salon friends and family, she started. Because it was true. As much as people said to keep a distance between yourself and your clients, Bernadette and Tate were family. There were people who'd been coming to her for her entire career. They might not be blood, but they were her family.

As you know, I was very close to my grandmother. She was with me from my very first pair of shears and she was an integral part of starting my own salon. Sadly, she passed away two weeks ago. My family announced it via this very site without calling me, which I'm sure shocks none of you. Vane Attraction *will be business as usual, although I will be taking some time to grieve. I will contact you if there is a change in your appointment. For the meantime, please enjoy my favorite picture of Gran. I know she was very proud of me and I'll love her forever.*

Vane added a photo of her and Gran from last Christmas. She'd been teaching her to use filters and they were both sporting little cartoon deer antlers. Gran looked super happy. She knew that Tammy, her aunt, would see the post and likely report back to her parents what she said. Which meant neighbors and friends of the family who followed the shop would know what they did. Vane closed the app and threw her phone on her bed. Enough of that. She had clients to reschedule and a new girlfriend to dress up for.

Or a girl that she would very much like to be girlfriends with. Or something like that.

Vane stood in line at Devil's, waiting to get Hannah a hot cocoa before she went to work. Tate was at one of the high tops, grinning smugly.

"Oh, fuck," Quita said as she took Vane's order. "Tate won."

"Yeah, but you got the bonus points," Tate said. Quita shrugged.

"Bonus points?" Vane asked. Quita smiled.

"Tate bet it would take you two this long, but I bet you'd come in marked to high hell. Didn't you notice that Hannah's a biter?"

Vane had not, in fact, noticed. She'd been in too much of a rush to get ready and see Hannah that she hadn't really even looked in the mirror. She didn't want to know what her hair looked like. She shrugged. "Does it really surprise you that I might like it that way?"

Tate scowled. "Ew."

"That's what you get for asking questions you don't want to know the answer to, kid," Vane said. She looked over at Quita. "How are you doing? You seemed upset last night."

"Jesse and I talked a bit, so I'm feeling better. I'm going to try to work on this purpose or passion or whatever thing Eve is pushing. The collective 'they' are going to ask Eve about doing a play here," Quita said. She shrugged again. "It will be what it will be."

"It will be perfectly fine," Vane promised her. She moved to the other end of the bar to wait for Frankie, the part-timer who filled in when they were short, to make the drinks. It was always a toss-up as to whether she was going to make what you ordered. Vane thanked her, and left Tate and Quita to their bickering about where the stage should be in the coffee shop. She tried hard to look cool, sauntering into her shop while carrying two beverages. Shit, she should've brought Bex one to soothe her over her lost bet. Oh well. She'd buy them all lunch or something. She was just on the verge of spilling the coffees trying to get the knob twisted when the door opened from the other side and Hannah smiled at her, although it was partially covered up by her mask. It was a genuine, sweet 'happy to see you' smile that made butterflies erupt in Vane's stomach. Vane grinned back.

She held out the cocoa.

"Got you this."

Hannah's eyes were bright and shining. "Thank you, dearest."

ABOUT THE AUTHOR

Avery Morstan

Avery Morstan is a non-binary actor, designer & writer living in rural Maryland with dreams of moving closer to, well, anywhere. When they are not busy telling people how great it was that one time they lived in Philadelphia, they are sewing for their YouTube channel (Mad Rabbit Society), performing on stages in and around the DC area and cheerfully terrorizing thrift stores throughout Maryland and Pennsylvania. Their exploits can be found on their Instagram, TikTok and YouTube accounts -
@madrabbitsociety & @AveryMorstan.

BOOKS IN THIS SERIES

Quaint City Sweet Romance

Set in the rural mountains of Maryland, Quaint City has all the tropes a romantic tourist could want. From witty banter at the local coffee shop, Devil's Stomping Ground, to a sweet jaunt through the local farmer's market- where you just might meet a frenemie that becomes your future crush- Q.C. has it all.

Seams A Bit Queer

Upcycle My Heart

Vane Attraction

Falling For Apple

Best Worst Prize (June 2023)

BOOKS IN THIS SERIES

Quaint City After Dark

Feeling a little bloodthirsty after all that sweet stuff? Consider finding out what happens when the sun goes down in Quaint City. Visit the Cabin, a log cabin gay club on the weekend, vampire hangout on the week nights, where you can buy your beer or your blood on tap.

The Vampire & Mr. Claus

Carmilla '86